About the Author

Jessica Tebow is a book-loving, video-gaming nerd who loves to ride horses and garden. She likes to read any type of book, but fantasy is her favorite genre.

Questor's Emporium

Jessica Tebow

Questor's Emporium

Olympia Publishers
London

www.olympiapublishers.com
OLYMPIA PAPERBACK EDITION

Copyright © Jessica Tebow 2024

The right of Jessica Tebow to be identified as author of
this work has been asserted in accordance with sections 77 and 78 of
the Copyright, Designs and Patents Act 1988.

All Rights Reserved

No reproduction, copy or transmission of this publication
may be made without written permission.
No paragraph of this publication may be reproduced,
copied or transmitted save with the written permission of the publisher,
or in accordance with the provisions
of the Copyright Act 1956 (as amended).

Any person who commits any unauthorised act in relation to
this publication may be liable to criminal
prosecution and civil claims for damage.

A CIP catalogue record for this title is
available from the British Library.

ISBN: 978-1-80439-736-7

This is a work of fiction.
Names, characters, places and incidents originate from the writer's
imagination. Any resemblance to actual persons, living or dead, is
purely coincidental.

First Published in 2024

Olympia Publishers
Tallis House
2 Tallis Street
London
EC4Y 0AB

Printed in Great Britain

Dedication

I dedicate this book to those who believed in me and to those who said I would fail.

I also dedicate this book to my father. He would have been so proud. I love and miss you every day.

Prologue

In Sehill, a country where magic and mystical creatures run wild across the land, a handsome black carriage moves through the night. A storm is brewing on the horizon as they make their way to an inn. The creaking of wheels and the jingle of tack on the horses are the only sounds that can be heard. The two occupants inside the carriage do not speak, one by choice and the other forbidden. A man looks boredly down at the woman kneeling on the floor. She has been there for hours, waiting to be allowed to get up. Today, it seems, she must stay on the hard floor. It has been like this for five days. Five long, grueling days of kneeling on the carriage floor. Of being forced to not speak or move, no matter the discomfort. But when they stop, the nights are worse. The man either leaves her to sleep on the floor, or she becomes his plaything on which to enact his sadistic fantasies.

It's always the same. The beatings, the chains, and shackles. Starvation is his new favorite game to play with her. She can eat only when he does, and only when he says. The last time she has eaten was three days ago, forced to watch him as he sat across from her and ate his fill. The shortest period of his starvation game so far. Other times, he has forced her to go almost a full week with just a stale crust of bread and some water now and then, if she was lucky. She fears she will not last much longer. She can feel how loose her clothing has become on her now sickly slim frame. Just hanging off her boney shoulders. What was supposed to be a happy marriage, regardless if it was arranged or not, has turned into a living nightmare. The woman knows once they reach his home in the countryside, away from prying eyes, her treatment will become worse. If that is even possible. For three years, she has been with this monster in a man's skin. He hid it so well the first year, playing the loving husband. But it was all for show to fool everyone, even her parents. Slowly, he showed his true colors. A casual slap here, and foul name thrown her way there. Through the years, it has escalated. Soon, he will kill her either by accident while playing one of his sick "games" or on purpose when he finally gets bored with her.

But she must escape, and soon. She has been slowly forming a plan ever since she found out where they are headed, and tonight is her last hope of escape. She has stored a small bag of the meager belongings he has not taken from her under the seat in the carriage. A few small books her father gave her when she was younger. Some jewelry he made her wear whenever he would host one of his Senator parties. Then finally, a handful of gold coins she stole from his study whenever she could without being noticed. Nothing else, because she doesn't want anything to slow her down when she makes a run for it.

She tilts her head up just slightly enough so she can see the face of her husband and startles when she finds him staring down at her. His cruel brown eyes survey her as a sadistic smile plays across his face, making his normally square features sharper, more predatory. He lifts his hand and sweeps his black hair out of his eyes as he continues to stare at her.

"Well, my dear," he purrs in his sickly sweet voice. That voice means pain is coming. "I have been feeling bored for the past hour and need some entertainment. When we stop for the night, I want you to freshen up before you come into the inn. I have a dress ready for you under my seat. Pity it will not last long, though." He leers at her as he pulls a small satchel towards him from its place on the floor beside her.

In the satchel, she can hear the clinking of chains. He pulls out a tight metal collar and some shackles. The woman knows what is coming next. She will dress up like a doll for him, and then he will destroy the dress by beating her and tearing it to shreds with his whip. Nothing good will come tonight when he seeks his entertainment from her. But this is the chance she has been hoping for. He has never left her alone to change before on this trip. Always watching, never letting her stray too far. This is the chance she has been waiting for, the moment she will escape. She will pretend to put on whatever poor excuse of fabric he calls a dress and slip away.

"Yes," he continues, none the wiser of her scheming. "I think we will try something new tonight. Tell me, dear, what are your thoughts on candles?"

"I do not know what you mean, my Lord," she says, keeping her eyes downcast the way he likes.

"Why, I will pour hot wax all over you, and run the flame near your skin, of course. I hear it is quite stimulating. I wonder, though, how hot must the wax be, and how close to the skin one can tolerate the flame?" he muses as he leers at her, his nasty smile growing darker.

She does not answer after that. So, his plan is to burn her tonight. That is something new. He usually either binds her, beats her, or a variety of both. She does not want to find out what he really wants to do with the candle.

She feels the slight lurch of the carriage as it pulls to a stop and knows her time has run out. It was now or never. She just has to time it perfectly, and make sure everyone is distracted so she can run.

"Now, my dear, I will run inside and get a room. Don't keep me waiting," he warns as he steps down from the carriage and makes his way to the inn.

She waits a moment or two more, then reaches under the seat where she has stored her satchel of belongings. Next, she opens the other seat and pulls out the sorry excuse for a dress. It is a vulgar thing, made of red lace and almost completely see through. He forced her to wear these types of dresses and parade her around in them on this trip just to humiliate her, treating her worse than a common whore. He treats whores better than her; she knows, because he would bring them to his house in the senate and make her watch as he bedded them.

Stuffing the scrap of a dress into her satchel as well—she may need it later either to sell it or make bandages. Anything but wearing the damned thing. Maybe burn it for warmth. Smiling ruefully at the thought of burning it, she quickly makes her way out of the carriage. The driver is walking the horses to the stable and has not noticed her exiting. She silently slinks around the back of the inn and then takes off running into the night.

About an hour later, her husband storms out to the carriage, furious that he was kept waiting. He thought he had beaten that out of her. But he guesses he will have to remind her tonight about the consequences of keeping him waiting. Ripping the carriage door open, he finds her gone. Stunned for a moment, he lets out a dark chuckle as he runs his fingers through his hair.

"So, this is how she wants to play our game tonight," he thinks to himself. *"She has nowhere to go, and with a storm brewing, she will come crawling back soon enough."*

He turns around and heads back toward the inn to wait for her. But as he enters the inn, he spots one of his new men sitting in the corner with his large black wolf familiar and gets an idea. Motioning for him to come over, he speaks when the man nears.

"It seems my wife has taken a nighttime stroll. Find her and monitor her. Report to me when she is spotted and watch her but nothing more. Let's see what she does with her newfound freedom."

"Yes, sir," the man says in a reedy voice.

The man and his wolf walk out and disappear into the night.

Chapter 1
~ One Year Later ~

On the east side of Sehill, there is a village called Lancegate. It is near the Shrouded Woods. A petite, fair-skinned woman is setting her table up near a community bulletin board. Her shoulder-length, wavy, chocolate-colored hair shines in the sun as she is getting ready to sell anything she can for the day. Placing the last of her potions out, the woman feels a spark of excitement. Today is the day she hopes to sell something, and being near the bulletin board is the perfect place to be. Because that is where a person looking for a quest would go to pick up a job or bounty. With luck, they will buy something from her when they get their job off the board.

Rearranging her wares one last time, a loud commotion catches her attention. Now, this is nothing unusual, for rangers, mages, and warriors often pass through, coming to and from wherever their quest or mission takes them. For a small village, it is busy. It lies just between the wilderness, where most of the work is needed, and the capital of Inaslas, where the bounty is collected. But what is unusual today is the small creature barreling toward her at top speed. It is a weird little critter, small, about three feet tall, with greenish-brown skin and long pointy ears that poke out of a ridiculously enormous hat on its head. The woman gathers these details before it flips her table over when it collides with it, breaking most of the glass bottles she has just set on the table moments ago.

She watches as all her little potions leak into the ground in dismay. The small creature sits up, and adjusting the hat that had gone wayward on its head from the collision, smiles up at her. It is a male swamp goblin, known for their enchantment of plants and water, as well as their mischief magic. Like imitation and shadow magic. It is strange to see one here in this village, for swamp goblins live further west in the wetlands of the Venom Bog.

Standing up, it dusts itself off and adjusts its clothing as the person, a human chasing after it, reaches her table too. They look to be a warrior mage, and a furious one. The mage is tall and stocky in build, built like a bull, but with more fat than muscle. He has greasy, muddy brown hair, is slicked back into a ratty ponytail.

He glares first at the creature, then at the woman who is now unfortunately standing in front of the goblin, and bellows, "Out of the way!"

"Why would I do that? This is my table and I have a right to be here. Why should I move?" the woman snaps back, feeling irritated that the mage is yelling at her for no other reason than standing in front of him. She cleans up the potion bottles scattered all over the ground while trying to ignore him.

"Maybe he will go away and leave me alone if I just ignore him," she thinks to herself, turning her back on him.

"I need him to give back what he has stolen from me."

She turns to look at the suspect in question. The little bastard has the gall to shrug his shoulders while he puts his hands behind his back and rocks back and forth on his heels as he watches the exchange.

"Look, I don't want any trouble. I'm just a potion seller, but if you have anything that belongs to this man, please just give it back to him," the woman pleads.

"But it was pretty, and I wanted it," says the little goblin. "And besides, he was using it wrong, anyway. You are supposed to put it in the palm of your glove and not wear it around your neck. How are you supposed to aim at something from your neck?"

"How would you know about such things? I don't see you as a crafter or enchanter," the warrior mage sneers down at him.

"All right, all right! Just give it back to him and you both leave me alone to clean up my table," she states, glaring at the goblin.

"Fine, here you go, sir. The aiming stone. Take it."

The little goblin hands the man a small red stone about the size of a robin's egg. As the man slips the leather string around his neck as he walks away, she sees a distinct smirk on the goblin's face. Shaking her head and wanting nothing more from this situation, she continues to clean up all the spilled potions and broken glass. It took hours for her to collect and make the potions. If she wants to replace the stock she lost, it would be a very long night of brewing.

"You know, none of this stuff you're selling is very good."

"You're still here! What do you know about potions? I thought goblins only did small enchantments?" she snaps, turning to look at the goblin, who is now pushing one of her unbroken bottles around with his foot.

"I can tell you have weak ingredients. What are they even for, minor cuts? This will not do at all!" he says, pocketing the bottle he was toeing around.

"What do you mean, weak ingredients! I grow them myself. And why would you care about them?" the woman asks, outraged, feeling her face heat of embarrassment.

Truth be told, she knows they are weak, but she didn't need someone she just met to tell her they are.

"You helped me out of a tight spot just now, and I want to return the favor. Come, show me your crafting station and I will help you," the goblin says, pocketing another one of her bottles.

"Stop that! Quit taking my stuff! If you want to help so badly, then come along. It's the least you could do for knocking over my table." Snatching the last bottle before he does, she slips it into her bag, and grabbing the now broken table, walks away from the bulletin board and back toward her home.

The little goblin, no higher than the woman's chest, skips along beside her, admiring something he is holding in his hands and humming to himself. The woman tries to ignore him until she notices what it is. It's the red stone he gave back to the warrior mage.

"Hey! I thought you gave that back. If you have it, then what did you just give him?" she asks, turning her head to look at him.

"Well, duh, I would not give it back to him! The stone that I gave him is just a cat turd enchanted to look like the aiming stone. He doesn't need it if he will not use it correctly. By the way, the name is Tinker, not 'hey.' What's your name?"

"It's Gwyneth, but you can call me Gwyn... Wait a minute, don't change the subject. Just because someone doesn't use something the way you want them to, doesn't mean you can just take it from them! How long until the enchantment on the fake stone wears off?"

"Well, let me see," he says, scratching his head. "I think about an hour until it turns back into a turd." He laughs. "It is going to be so hilarious when he looks down and sees a turd hanging from his neck and not the stone!"

At this point, he is rolling on the ground laughing, and Gwyn just ignores him and keeps walking.

"And," he says as he continues to laugh, getting up and following her once again, "I set another enchantment. It will be stuck to his chest longer after it turns!" He wipes a tear from his eye from laughing so hard.

She is now thinking that she has made a huge mistake in letting him tag along with her. With him around, she knows there will be trouble to follow, and trouble is not something she needs. It has taken her a year to make herself a quiet life in this small village, and she doesn't need this goblin stirring it up and ruining it.

But it is too late now, and within a few minutes they are already outside of the small village and walking down the main road toward the edge of the woods nearby. Once they get to the woods, they continue walking through the trees. After about five minutes of walking on a small dirt path, they come up to Gwyn's home.

It is a small, round cottage that was abandoned when she found it. It has cute little square windows in the front to let in light, and a small sloping thatched roof with a chimney poking out of the side. Behind the cottage is a small garden with herbs and vegetables growing in it. The side of the cottage has a small bee-keeping box with flowers planted all around. Between two trees is a clothesline for hanging laundry, and there is a pile of logs stacked against the cottage wall. It was an old hunting cottage, long forgotten and abandoned. Gwyn had found it, cleaned it, and fixed it up as best she could, and now calls it home. It is small and comforting for a woman living alone to feel safe.

As she walks up to unlock the front door, Gwyn hears a sharp whistle behind her. With a laugh in his voice, she hears Tinker's opinion.

"What a shit shack!"

Chapter 2

Gwyn pauses at the door, registering what has just been said about her home. She can confront him about it, but then again, he has magic, and she does not. It is not like she doesn't want to confront him and defend her home, but she has learned not to fight back years ago. Her standing up to the mage was a rare occurrence. So, Gwyn ignores him and makes her way into the cottage. Inside, it is semi-square and small. With only one room which makes up the bedroom, kitchen, and eating area, with a small table by the back window where Gwyn does most of her potion making. There is a cozy hearth with a large pot bubbling softly on the left wall. She has her bed tucked into the far back corner of the right side. A little nightstand holds a small stack of books on it. On the other end, a line for hanging her clothes in the winter or during the stormy season, with a sheet hanging on it.

She walks over to the table and sets down the bag of salvaged potions, and starts setting them out for Tinker to inspect. He said he would help her as payment, so he might as well start with the ones she already has and see how they could improve. Pulling the last potion out, there isn't much left from the crash from earlier.

"So much for all my hard work," she thinks to herself, shaking her head and sighing.

Truth be told, Gwyn could sell none of the stuff she made. The elixirs for minor aches, yes sometimes, but not the actual potions for healing. Like Tinker said, they are just no good. If she wants to be a good potion maker and seller, she needs to change it up and if he's willing to help her, then all the better. She can learn from this and become a better potion maker, if not a novice alchemist, and soon have something people would want to actually buy. Gwyn is a great herbalist, but as for knowing what magic ingredient to put in the potions, she doesn't have a clue.

While Gwyn is setting the potions up for his inspection, Tinker walks around her place, snooping around. He stops at the giant pot she has hanging on the hearth and pulls the lid off to inspect what is inside.

"What is this in here?" he says with a grimace on his face, returning the lid.

"That is our dinner. To be more exact, it is rabbit stew, with potatoes and a hint of rosemary to give it a bit of flavor. I need to add salt to it in just a moment, but while I tend to that, look at these potions and see what you can do."

As she walks over to the stew and starts stirring it, he just stares at her for a moment, studying her, then turns to the table where the potions sit. Gwyn hears him murmuring to himself as she adds the salt, tasting it as she goes. Satisfied that the stew is ready for them when dinner time comes, she looks at him to see what he thinks of the potions.

"What are you doing?" Gwyn asks him, seeing that he has not only opened the bottles but has tasted them as well.

"I am trying them out," he says with a frown, "So, these are not all that bad. You have the basics down, but don't have a key ingredient to make it potent enough to work the way you want them to. These are great for common stuff like coughs and mild pain, but if you want to make a healing potion, you need a secret ingredient that does the job for you."

"But I don't know any sort of magic or what type of magic

ingredient to put in it," she says, looking at the bottle and wondering what she should use to put in them.

"Well, that's what you have me for, isn't it? Now show me the garden you used to get your ingredients from. I assume you grow them yourself?" he says hopping down off his chair and walking over to Gwyn.

"Yes, I like to make sure my ingredients are fresh and not tampered with. You never know what you are really getting when you purchase ingredients from sellers."

Gwyn leads him outside to the back of her cottage and shows him her garden. It has many herbs and plants that she has researched and used in the past for the failed potions that were made. She even has a few exotic plants, like a quick seed bush she collected and grew herself. She gives him a moment to look around and study the different plants. While he does, Gwyn looks around as well to see if there are any other plants she needs for her work. There is always a new plant she can add to her garden, whether for eating or for potion making.

"This is very impressive!" he exclaims. "We will not need much of anything in the way of plants, maybe an odd one here or there, but I can see great potential here."

"Thank you. So, what do you suggest I use for the potions to make them better?" she asks, putting her hands on her hips and staring down at him.

"I'm glad you asked that question, but first, let's go inside and eat. I haven't eaten in a few days, and I am starving, even if it is nasty rabbit stew."

"You don't eat rabbit?"

"No, I eat vegetables and seafood, but not red meat. But I'm so hungry, I'll eat anything," he says as his stomach growls, proving his point.

They both walk into the cottage and Tinker sits down at the small table, his legs swinging back-and-forth, humming to himself. It is then that Gwyn gets a good, close look at him. To add on to her earlier assessment, his clothes are very shabby, a large green hat, a small leather vest with a white shirt underneath, and brown linen shorts. All of them are very dirty and in desperate need of repairs, or to just throw them away. As Gwyn ladles the food for them, she asks him about his clothes, and if he wants her to repair and wash them.

"No, sorry, Gwynie, these are the only pair of clothes I have," he says, taking the bowl of stew from her and eating as fast as he can, even though it is still steaming.

"Slow down! It's not going anywhere. You will burn your mouth."

Watching him eat, Gwyn thinks for a moment about what he said, and it hits her. She has an old set of shirts and pants that are too thin and worn for her now that she was just going to turn into rags. Setting her own bowl down, Gwyn walks over to her bed and grabbing the box underneath that has all the extra clothes in it, she fishes out the pair in question. He stops shoveling food into his mouth for a moment and looks at the clothes in her hand.

"What are you doing?"

"I am giving you these clothes; I don't need them, and they are too old for me now. You can put them on, and I can hem the length to fit you and wash the others, too," Gwyn says, digging around under the bed for her sewing kit and washing stuff.

"But why? What's in it for you to do this?" he asks, suspicious now as he gets up from the table. "No one ever does anything without wanting something in return, and no one EVER does anything nice to goblins. People hate and mistrust us for our powers and our way of living."

"Yeah, well, I'm not just anybody. We are going to be partners, right? It is a fair trade you get these. I'm not using them, and they are just going to waste under my bed, so you can wear them. It's just as simple as that, no strings attached or secret motives to it. I'm just trying to do something nice. But if you don't want them, I can just rip them up and use them for rags."

"Well now, if you are just going to rip them up, I will take them. No sense in a good pair of clothes going to waste," he says, grabbing the clothes out of her hand. "I like the color. Red is my favorite. And is this material wool? It will feel nice and warm in the coming cold months. Are these pants buckskin? It's a nice deep brown color, and it is so soft."

On all accounts, he is right. Both articles of clothing are too small for her now. But it reminds her that winter is coming and that she will need new, warmer clothing if she wants to survive another winter in her small cottage. Taking the clothes back from him, Gwyn holds up the pants to his side and then the wool shirt, to get a sense of how much will need to be cut off and hemmed. After the measurements are done, Gwyn tells him to hand her his hat and vest so that she can mend them as well. Tinker hands them to her without question and sits back down to finish his dinner. He now eats her bowl of stew too, along with the last of the bread she has. She sets to work at hemming the legs of the pants and sets his hat and vest in the washing bin. Setting another large stew pot beside the one that had their dinner in it and heats some rainwater that she has collected in a barrel for just this purpose. With the pants and shirt done being mended, he gets up to fill his bowl with a third helping of the stew. She hands him the hemmed clothes and tells him to go change behind the sheet she has hanging in the corner. She refills her bowl so she can finally eat.

As he comes back around with the new clothes on, he looks

at Gwyn for a moment, then thanks her.

"I have never known humans to be kind to me. Thank you for the clothes and the meal. It is the first time on my own since I was run off from my clan. I am a weak male, and they frowned upon males that tend to the herbs and medicine or any other female work like I have done," he says, looking down at his feet. "I have little magic in me, unlike most of the other males in my clan, so my mother thought I could be of use in the herb gardens and with the healers. But it turns out it was a greater embarrassment to my father, so he ran me out of the clan. Now here I am all alone and with nothing to me but weak magic."

"So, they kicked you out just for trying to be useful?" she says, shaking her head in disbelief.

"Yes. They saw it as me not trying hard enough to strengthen my magic and just wasting away my days with the plants and flowers being lazy. Also, they did not like me being around all the unmated females learning the craft as well."

"Well, they do not know what they are missing. How about this? If I make it big, you can go rub it in your clan's face about how wrong they were about you."

He just nods his head and stares at the potion bottles left on the table from earlier. Gwyn does not know how to help him when she can't even help herself. By giving him the last warm set of clothing, she now has no more warm clothes for herself, let alone food stored up for the winter that could feed two. But she hopes in the future she can give him more than just a few pieces of clothing and a weak stew. To do that, Gwyn needs to ask him how to make something that people will want to buy. She thinks for a moment about what is missing in the potion. He said she was close, and it was just missing something. But what was it?

"What do you think my healing potions need in order to be better?"

"Unicorn poop."

"Excuse me?" Gwyn asks, looking confused at him as he grins, which is a very unsettling sight with his frog-like mouth.

"We need unicorn poop. The animal itself has healing powers. It can use its horn to purify water and heal other members of its herd," he says as he paces.

"As it is illegal to hunt or kill them or take their horns, we can use other means, such as their waste, to get their power. It goes through the body and picks up small bits of healing magic. We can cook it down, press it for the juices, and make a salve or potion out of it."

"But that's disgusting!" she exclaims, setting her spoon down, no longer interested in the stew. "Why would anyone use poop for an ingredient?"

"Well, I heard that some rich humans drink a black liquid that wakes them up and makes them hyper that they brew from cat poop. Why not do the same thing, but make a salve or potion out of it instead with unicorn poop?" Tinker says, stopping his pacing to stare at her.

"Hyper drink? Do you mean coffee? People make coffee out of cat shit? Where?"

"There are some people who live in a jungle that make it and then sell it to the rich." He paces again as he speaks. "We will worry about that later. We first need to locate where the unicorns are. Where they are is where we will find the poop. Any suggestions?"

"The closest place to find them, if I remember correctly, is the Crystal River. It is one of the few locations where they live," Gwyn says, getting up from the table with her bowl of stew. She isn't starving any more with all this talk of poop.

She pours her stew into the stew pot and pulls the other pot she has heated for Tinker's dirty clothes. As Gwyn puts his clothes into the pot to soak, she turns back to Tinker.

"Now, the Crystal River is about four miles west from here

through the Shrouded Woods. Lucky for us, my cottage is just inside the edge of the Shrouded Woods. It is not a very safe journey, though."

"Four miles is nothing if we keep a steady pace. We can make it to the river by nightfall if we start out first thing in the morning. Once we get there, we can make camp, collect the poop the following morning, and then be back by nightfall," Tinker says with an excited smile. "Besides, what is the worst that could happen?"

Gwyn says nothing while continuing to clean his clothes. Thinking about what he said and the journey she now has to prepare for, she sets about washing and hanging them out to dry by the fire so they will be ready by morning for him. After that, she gathers supplies for their trip in the morning. Grabbing a large travel satchel, she puts some hard cheese in it for them to eat along with some berries, while also filling two large water skins. She then puts a compass and her fire starter inside. Next, she puts a smaller satchel inside to put the collected poop in.

Gwyn pulls out a bedroll and then a spare blanket so she can make Tinker a bed to sleep on for the night.

"When I get back, I will have to make a more permanent solution for his sleeping arrangements," she thinks to herself.

She hopes that the plan he came up with is as easy as it sounds. But Gwyn gets the feeling he had just jinxed them both with his last statement. Going behind the curtain herself, she changes into a sleeping gown and gets ready for bed. Coming back around and going to a small washbasin, she cleans her face and turns to him.

"I hope we can pull this off. But I guess we will have to see when we get there. Good night, Tinker. I'm sorry that I only have this blanket, but I hope you sleep well, and see you in the morning."

Gwyn blows the candle out on the small nightstand by her

bed and lays down for the night. All is quiet, save for the soft rustle of Tinker settling into the blanket on the floor.

"I hope I have made the right choice to trust him," Gwyn thinks to herself. *"I just met him and now I am letting him sleep in my cottage with me. For all I know, he could wait for me to go to sleep and then rob me blind like he did that guy from earlier. Or worse, he could kill me in my sleep. But I think it is time for me to trust people again. I will see in the morning if he is worth trusting."*

As she turns in her bed to get more comfortable, she hears Tinker say, "Good night, Gwynie."

Chapter 3

Dawn comes early, with Gwyn having gotten little sleep. She awoke to every little noise or movement. But Tinker stayed on his spot and slept all night. She sits up and stretches her tired, stiff limbs, then tries to rub the sleep from her eyes. Getting up and stoking the dying coals in the grate, she tries to reheat the stew for breakfast. Pulling Tinker's clothes off the drying rack, she folds them, then sets them on the table.

"I will find a better place for them when we get back from our little adventure," she thinks to herself.

As she pours two bowls of stew for herself and Tinker, she hears him stir. He looks more rested than her and is ready for the trek. Grumbling a low, "Morning," and taking his bowl, he sits at the table and eats. He stops for a moment, then he reaches into his pocket and turns to Gwyn, holding out his hand.

"Here. You can have this for showing me such kindness."

It is the little red stone from yesterday that he had stolen.

"I can't take that. It's not mine. Besides, I have no use for aiming stones. I have no bow or other weapon to use it with."

"Oh Gwynie! Don't be silly. Take it. We can get you a bow later for it. But for now, take it and put it in the palm of a glove, just in case. I know a little magic, but you have nothing, so here!" he says, shoving the stone at her. She takes the stone from him and goes to the pack she had prepared the night before. But she stops, instead grabbing a glove and putting it on her right hand. Next, she puts the stone on her palm inside the glove. Making sure it is secure, she shows him and he nods his head in approval.

"Might as well get used to having it, even though I don't plan on using it," Gwyn thinks as she checks her pack one more time.

After they finish their breakfast, Gwyn puts the fire out in the grate, and they walk out the front door. Locking the door, Gwyn turns to him and asks.

"Well, you ready for this?"

"Of course! I'm excited about getting this adventure started," he exclaims with a huge smile on his face.

She looks at him and shakes her head, but smiles at his enthusiasm. They turn west, following the compass, and start off through the trees that connect to the Shrouded Woods. They are a mix of oak and birch trees with deep green leaves, and dense firs with bundles of dark needles, wrapped in layers of mist. This is how Shrouded Woods gets its name, from the very mist that flows through it. Thin mist lies along the edges of the woods, but thickens closer to the middle. No one knows where the mist comes from, but the Shrouded Woods are the only place like it. During the first few hours, they walk in silence with Gwyn in the lead, making a slow but steady trek through the trees. The further they walk, the darker the surrounding woods get, and the harder it becomes to see through the mist, thickening with every step. As the hours tick by and it gets closer to midday, they stop for a brief break of berries and cheese.

After the break, the companions continue to walk further into the woods. The journey is taking longer than she thought. *"I cannot remember the last time I have walked this long,"* Gwyn thinks as she picks her way through the roots and underbrush.

The mist is thinning a bit, and there is a faint sound of running water in the distance. Gwyn feels like if they get any closer, they might scare the unicorns away, and since the sun is now setting, they decide to set up camp. Setting down her satchel, she looks to Tinker.

"Okay, so we are very close to the river, Tinker. I think it is best we set camp here for the night and collect the poop at first light. I can make us a small fire if you want to get some firewood. But do not go too far. It will be hard to find each other in this mist."

"Sure, Gwynie. I will whistle as I collect wood, so that you can hear me and know where I am," he says as he walks off into the mist.

Gwyn collects small kindling and leaves to start the fire while she waits for Tinker to come back with the firewood. All the while, she hears Tinker's sharp whistles. She gets the fire started with the sticks around camp and continues to listen; she can no longer hear Tinker.

"Where did he go? I hope he didn't go too far," Gwyn thinks to herself as she keeps the embers burning.

Waiting to hear from him, she gets out the last of the berries and the cheese. She hears a low, sharp whistle. It is very faint but getting closer.

She sets about cutting the cheese and putting berries into the middle. Setting it close to the fire, she warms the berry-filled cheese up when Tinker walks up to her through the mist.

"Gwynie, there were a lot of poops near the river. I went to check it out and I think we will get a good haul from this."

"You can see it in this darkness?" she asks him while handing him a gooey mess of food.

"Yeah, I can see in the dark a little better than a human. This will be easy. We can experiment with the poop for the best healing salve."

After they eat, Gwyn and Tinker both lay down by the fire for the night. Watching the fire burn low, Gwyn feels the tiny hairs on the back of her neck stand up, and gets the strong feeling of something watching her. Try as she might to ignore it, the feeling keeps her awake most of the night. Tossing and turning, she falls asleep in the early hours of the morning.

Dawn comes, finding her yet again exhausted and on edge after two nights of little sleep. She glances over at Tinker, who has scooted closer to her in the night, looking as tired as she is.

"Did you not get any sleep either?" Gwyn asks him while trying to hold back a yawn.

"No, not at all, Gwynie. I felt like I was being watched, but when I looked around, nothing was there."

"Same for me, too. Maybe the mist in these woods is playing tricks on us. There are mist bears said to roam these woods," she says as she cleans up camp.

"The sooner we got out of the woods, the better. I was never one to walk in the woods and being in the Shrouded Woods with no protection or weapons is feeling like a stupid idea. We need to hurry to the river and get what we came for, lest we run into trouble," Gwyn worries to herself.

Moving about the campsite, Gwyn makes sure the fire is all the way out as Tinker goes ahead of her to the river. Grabbing the collection bag out of her satchel, she holds it in one hand and slings the bigger satchel over her shoulder. She makes her way toward the river, being careful to not step on anything that will make too much noise. Gasping at the sight that meets her when she gets there is breathtaking. True to its name, the Crystal River looks like a ribbon of crystalized water cutting through the woods. It shimmers in every color of the rainbow and sparkles when the sun hits it, like a living kaleidoscope. It is the most beautiful sight Gwyn has ever seen. Going up to it, she pauses to just watch the river move and wonders how such a river came to be.

There is a legend about the river that she has heard about, that states it is the blood of some giant god who fought and lost in a battle long ago. Looking at it now, Gwyn can't help but think it is true. Something so strange yet beautiful must come from some unknown or cosmic origin. Other tales say it is the unicorns themselves that turn the river crystal-like with their magic, as they bless and purify the water before they drink it. Regardless of how it came to be, they are there for poop and not to look at the water.

Gwyn starts by looking around for the poop of a unicorn. It is very similar to that of horses, but somewhat smaller. She sees the small piles here and there and begins putting some into the bag. *"I never thought I would pick up animal poop, but if Tinker said it will work, I must at least try it, regardless of how gross it is. I hope this will help make a healing potion and not be one of his goblin tricks."* Gwyn grimaces to herself as she continues picking up the poop.

As they are collecting the poop, Gwyn gets that uneasy feeling of being watched again. She looks around, and with a start, she sees him in the mist's shadow. The unicorn is slender in build, like a deer with the head of a horse; he has a long but scraggly beard on his chin, and a long slender tail; almost like a donkey, but longer, with it reaching the ground and having the long hairs feathering out from the sides with a slight curl at the tip. His coat is pearlescent with an almost shiny hue to it. The horn on his head is about two feet long, but it has chips missing from it from past battles. The stallion is old, judging by the horn and the scraggly beard.

He just stares at her for a moment before he rotates his delicate ears in Tinker's direction. Tinker, not knowing that the unicorn is watching him, continues to pick through the poop for the freshest to take back with them.

"Tinker!" Gwyn whisper-shouts to him.

"What, Gwynie? Why are you whispering?" he says, turning to look at me.

As he turns, he catches sight of the unicorn and freezes. The stallion is now looking at him with his ears pinned back. Tinker turns to look at Gwyn slowly, then looks back again at the stallion. He takes a step back toward Gwyn while still facing the stallion.

"Stop!" Gwyn warns him, but he just smiles at her and keeps backing toward her.

When he has almost reached her, he takes a step back and when he does; he steps on a twig, snapping it under his foot. Upon hearing the snap, the unicorn peels back his lips and bares his teeth while he lowers his head with his horn aimed at them.

"It's okay, Gwynie," Tinker says to her, "he will not harm you because unicorns do not harm maidens."

At the sound of his voice, the unicorn charges at them, and they run for it. The stallion is not happy to find strange creatures in his territory. He is hot on their heels as they tear through the woods, weaving through the trees to slow the unicorn down from his chase. As fast and as agile as a unicorn can be, a tree could damage or break the horn. And then the unicorn would lose all its magic, so the stallion slows as they run through a dense set of trees to throw him off. After a moment more of the chase, the stallion slows down and turns back the way it had come toward the river.

Hiding behind a large tree and breathing heavily, Gwyn glares at Tinker.

"Why did you keep moving towards me with it watching you?" she says crossly, asking him. "It could have killed us."

"I thought because you are a maiden, he would not charge us. I guess the legends are not true about unicorns being gentle towards them," he says with a shrug, "But you know what is worse than him charging us?"

"What?" Gwyn asks, moping the sweat off her brow and trying to steady her breathing.

"We dropped the bag of poop."

"We almost died, and you are worried about a bag of shit!" Gwyn screeches at him, unable to contain her anger. "What is wrong with you? Do you not care that it chased us down, and we almost died? If you would have stopped, like I said, he might have lost interest in us and moved on, but you just had to do what you wanted and put us both in danger. Do you take anything seriously?"

"That's not very nice, Gwyn," he says, flinching away and looking hurt. "It is the main reason we came here. Without it, we might as well not have come at all, and like I said, I thought he would not charge at us because you are a maiden. Now we must go back and get the bag so we can leave."

He walks back in the direction that they had run, and Gwyn stands there for a moment, watching him walk away. She feels guilty for exploding at him. It is not his fault that he doesn't know that she is not a maiden. She jogs to catch up with him and they walk together in a heavy silence back to the river. When they hear running water again, they creep toward the river, trying not to make a sound. When they reach the river, they both hide behind a tree and look around for any signs of the stallion.

It looks like the stallion has moved on, so they snatch up the bag of poop and start back home. But Gwyn stops and turns back toward the river.

"Do you have the potion bottles you took yesterday with

you?" she asks Tinker, while staring at the water.

He looks at Gwyn for a moment, and without a word, slips the bottle out of his pocket and hands it to her. Gwyn takes the bottle, and as she bends down, she takes the cork out of it and fills the bottle with the crystalized water from the river.

"You never know, it might help in our potion making."

Tinker just shrugs and turns to walk back to the cottage. Gwyn puts the cork back into the bottle and walks behind him home.

Chapter 4

As they make their way back to Gwyn's home, she can't stop thinking about how harshly she spoke to Tinker.

"I know it is not his fault that I am not a maiden or that he believed in the old stories about them. One thing is for sure, I must tell him why his idea didn't work and why I got so angry with him. But how should I start? How much should I tell him? Will he look at me with pity or disgust like everyone else I have told?" These are a few of the questions Gwyn always worries about whenever she tries to reveal her past. But if they are going to be partners, he must know about her past, like how he shared some of his.

Gwyn goes with just the short version, but now she must try to broach the subject.

"Hey, Tinker?"

"What Gwyneth?"

"Okay, so not a good start. He didn't even look at me and he said my entire name, which, if I think about it, is the first time he has done that," Gwyn thinks.

"I just wanted to say I'm sorry for how I talked to you earlier. I didn't have the right to yell at you like that. The old legend about unicorns falling docile to maidens is a long-standing myth."

He just keeps walking, saying nothing, but Gwyn knows he is listening to her. As she started talking, he turned his ear towards her while pretending to ignore her. So, she pushes on.

"Also, even if the myth was true, it never would have worked with me... because I am not a maiden, or at least I haven't been one in a long time."

"What do you mean? How can you not be a maiden?"

"Well, I am... I was married, and had a husband," she says, not looking him in the eye. Gwyn does not like to talk about her past. It is one of those things she wants to remain buried and forgotten.

"You mean like a mate?" he asks, while he tries to look her in the eye.

"Yes, in a way... I was—"

Before she can finish telling him, a terrible roar splits the air, and along with it, a faint sound of someone calling for help. It is hard to tell where it is coming from, but it sounds close. Gwyn turns to look at Tinker and he is staring to their left. His long ears help him pick up the location better than she can. He then turns to her and gives one look while nodding his head in the direction the roars are coming from, and takes off.

"Tinker, wait!" she calls to him as she tries to keep up.

He does not know what he is running towards, but Gwyn does. The only animal in these woods who could make that sound is a mist bear. They are huge, stocky beasts, standing up to seven feet at the shoulder on all fours with grayish-white fur to blend into the mist of the forest. They have an aggressive nature and are very territorial, with five-inch-long bronze claws that can take on a unicorn stallion in its prime and win. And the little goblin is running right towards it.

He would never stand a chance, but he keeps running toward the sound. When Gwyn catches up to him, she grabs his arm from behind. He has stopped at the edge of a clearing and is peeking around a tree, looking into it. In the clearing is the mist bear looking up at a tree and acting very frustrated. There is someone hanging halfway up the tree, just out of the bear's reach. The person is screaming for help and looking around while trying to hang onto the tree. The person spots them at the edge of the clearing, and that is when Gwyn notices it is a man, and that he has blood running down one of his arms.

"Please help me! It is trying to kill me!" he shouts, waving one arm in their direction.

Gwyn looks at Tinker, then around the clearing. There is a pack on the ground along with a spear near the man in the tree, and a bunch of rocks lying about. It gives her an idea, a very crazy and dangerous idea.

"Tinker," she whispers to get his attention. "See those rocks lying around? Maybe if we stay on the edge of the clearing out of sight and throw rocks at the bear to distract it, we can give that man enough time to get down and run away."

"I think that might work, Gwynie. You go around one way, and me the other, and we can throw the rocks on different sides."

"Okay, let's be careful." She gathers rocks and finds the best place to throw them.

When she reaches a suitable spot to throw rocks at the bear, she sees the bear reach up and almost snag the man's boot with its claws, just missing it by inches. Gwyn reels her arm back and throws her first rock as hard as she can, hitting the bear in the rear. With a loud snort, the bear turns toward her and lets out a deafening bellow. As it charges toward her, another rock hits it from the other side of the clearing, making it whirl in that direction. Gwyn throws another rock, so it does not charge Tinker. As they throw rocks at the bear, they move back and away from the tree that the man is in, giving him enough room to get down and escape.

The plan is working. The man climbs his way down out of

the tree when, about halfway, he slips and falls the rest of the way, making a loud thud when he lands. But the bear, enraged now from being pelted by rocks, turns toward the man, and stands up on its hind legs, towering over all of them. It lets out a mighty roar while swiping its front paws back and forth with rage. As soon as it sets back down on all fours, it charges at the man. The bear is almost upon him when Tinker darts out into the clearing, yelling and throwing rocks to get the bear away from the man. The tactic works, but a little too well. Now the bear is charging after Tinker.

    Gwyn rushes out of the woods shouting and throwing rocks. While out of the corner of her eye, she sees the man dive for Tinker, pulling him out of the bear's path at the last moment. Now the bear turns toward her, and trapping her in the clearing, it rushes towards her. She looks around and sees the discarded spear, and lunges for it. Grabbing the spear, Gwyn finds herself pinned against a tree now, holding the spear out in front of her, watching as the bear comes charging toward her. She knows these are her last moments. Crouching down and bracing the spear behind her against the tree, she feels her right hand move on its own and emit a faint, red glow. She looks at her hand just as the bear is upon her. When the bear reaches out with its mouth mid-lunge to grab her, it gets impaled through the mouth by the spear that is moved by the stone at the last moment. Still in motion with the spear in its mouth, it crashes into the tree and Gwyn. She feels the full impact of the crash and gets smashed into the tree, hitting her head. The moment her head hits the tree, everything goes dark.

Chapter 5

"Would you get the fuck off me?" Tinker shouts at the strange man who is now lying on top of him. Tinker does not understand why he had to tackle him to the ground. He was doing just fine distracting the bear and knew he could get out of the way in time. But the big mammoth had to smash him into the ground.

"Oh! I'm so sorry for crushing you, little guy. I just wanted to make sure you didn't get caught by the bear," the strange man says to Tinker.

"Little guy! I am a full-grown male, not some little guy," Tinker growls up at him. "How dare you insult me just because you are taller than me. Wait a second, where's Gwynie?" he says, looking around for his new friend, panicking.

He doesn't want to lose his new friend. Tinker looks around for where he last saw her throwing rocks, when he sees the bear lying near a tree with the sharp point of the spear sticking out of the back of its head. From that angle, he cannot see her pinned under the bear. So, he moves closer to the bear, being careful just in case it is still alive.

"Wait a moment, there. It might still be alive. Let me get my bow and put an arrow in its head just to make sure," the tall man says as he runs to his pack lying on the ground and retrieves his bow and an arrow.

The man walks close to the bear's head, draws back the arrow and lets it loose into the bear's skull. Then he reaches under the bear's jaw to check for a pulse. Finding none, he gives Tinker the okay to come close. When they are both examining the bear, Tinker sees a foot sticking out from under the bear. With a gasp, he shouts, "I found her! She is under the bear! It's squishing her. Help me move it!" Tinker grabs hold of the head and tugs it with all his strength.

The man goes to the bear's other side and while Tinker pulls, he pushes until they get the bear off Gwyn enough to pull her free. Once she is free, the man lays her down gently. Tinker notices blood coming from the back of her head.

"Oh, no!" Tinker cries. "Poor Gwynie, you are bleeding." Tinker pats her check as he turns her head to get a better view of the wound.

"It seems it has injured the maiden in her attempt to rescue me," the man said, reaching for his pack on the ground.

"She is not a maiden! Also, whatever you have in your bag will not help her."

"How dare you say she is not a maiden! How would you know the virtue of this young woman?"

"Because she told me so?" Tinker says, running to get the bag Gwyn dropped. Grabbing the bag with the poop, he rushes back to her side. He grabs a handful and smears it on her wound. Taking his shirt, he rips a long strip off and wraps it around her head. Next, he takes the waterskin and trickles some of it into her mouth. He pats her cheek while brushing her long chocolate brown hair out of her face.

Tinker is feeling anxious about her condition. Her skin, usually fair with a rosy hue, is now an ashy pale color, and she did not stir the whole time he was dressing her head wound. But he can't find anything else wrong with her. He looks at the man just standing there watching him and with a snap says, "Are you just going to stand there, you big oaf? Help me take her back home. We need to make a pallet so we can drag her back and care for the wound better."

With a nod, the man picks up long sticks and pulls the laces off his shirt and boots. He ties the long sticks together to make a small litter for them to lay Gwyn on and picks up all the discarded packs lying around the clearing. Next, he moves over to Gwyn's unconscious form, and gently picking her up, he eases her down onto the litter and places all the packs at her feet. Walking to the front of the litter, he grabs the two sticks sticking out of the front.

Looking at Tinker, he says, "Lead the way."

Tinker, grabbing the compass out of Gwyn's pack, turns toward east and begins walking back toward her cottage. As they make their way back towards Gwyn's home, now and then, the man stops and marks a tree.

"What are you doing, oaf?" Tinker asks after the dozenth time the man stops to mark a tree.

"I am leaving a trail to come back and collect the hide and meat from the bear. It would be a waste to leave the thing there to rot in the forest without at least honoring it by eating it and using its fur," the man says. "And it's Larson, not oaf, you scrawny pest!"

"Name's Tinker, not pest, and I am not scrawny! I am the perfect size for a goblin!" Tinker argues back. "Every time we stop, we are wasting more time in getting Gwynie home where she can be safe."

They continue to bicker all the way back to the cottage, not stopping once. The journey is long and hard, and they reach her home late that night. But once they get inside, they stop bickering and work together to care for Gwyn. Larson sets Gwyn on her bed and Tinker starts a fire in the hearth and sets a teakettle to heating. Next, he pulls the makeshift bandage off her head and examines the wound again. But when he looks at the wound, it is still there. He scratches his head in confusion.

"Why didn't it work? I don't understand. I heard it would heal wounds. What did I do wrong?" Tinker wrings his hands as thinks to himself, feeling distraught.

He rushes over to the teakettle whistling on the hearth and pulls it off. He adds some birch bark to the tea leaves and sets it on the table to steep. Meanwhile, Larson goes to the washbasin and pours fresh, warm water. Carrying it over to her bed, he grabs some cloth to clean Gwyn's head. But by the time he returns to her bed, Gwyn has awoken and tries to sit up, but fails and lies back down.

"What happened? Where am I?" Gwyn croaks, trying to clear her parched throat.

"Gwynie! You're awake!" Tinker screeches, bounding over to her with a steaming cup of tea in his hand. "Here, drink this. It will help. How do you feel? We brought you back to your shit shack. You were under the bear. I think you killed it with the spear. What happened?"

Wincing from the loud outburst, Gwyn takes the tea from him, taking a tentative sip of the hot beverage. She makes a face when she tastes the bitter birch bark. Her head is pounding, with her feeling woozy, and she feels stiff all over. But it gets her thinking of other ingredients she could add to the healing potion. If it just healed the wound, but did not take the pain away, then she would have to see which of the herbs she had that would be best to pair with it. Looking at her tea, she gets an idea. What if she could add either birch bark or rosemary for pain, along with maybe comfrey to help heal? Or a mixture of several. She has most of what she needs in her garden. All she needs to do now is figure out how to combine it with their new special ingredient.

She tries to sit up again, but the room starts spinning, so she lies back down.

"The last thing I remember was the bear charging at me, then at the last moment, I felt my hand holding the spear move on its own and a faint red glow. Then I felt the impact of the bear slamming into me, but nothing after that. And please stop calling it that. It's a small cottage," Gwyn says, setting her drink down on the nightstand.

"I tried the poop on your wound, and it didn't work. I'm sorry, Gwynie," Tinker says, looking worried and wringing the cloth in his hand.

"You did what?" Gwyn asks, reaching up to the back of her head where most of the pain is coming from.

She feels a squishy substance smeared on the back of her head. Pulling her hand back, she looks down and sees that it is the poop they had collected. She first wonders why it didn't work to heal her, then she gets grossed out by that fact that she has shit smeared all over the back of her head.

"Tinker, why?" is the only thing she could ask him as she wipes her hands on the cloth he hands her.

"I thought it would work. It was supposed to work. I don't understand what happened."

"What was it he put on your wound?" The man speaks up from where he is standing in the corner.

"Oh, you're here too! Are you okay? Who are you?" Gwyn says, pulling the covers up to her chin and eyeing the man that they had saved.

She is very wary of him being so near her. But looking at him, sees that he is very handsome. At six feet, he is very tall, but not lanky. He has strong, broad shoulders and a wide chest. He has fair skin has tanned from being in the sun. His hair is a dark red that is almost brown, and his deep blue eyes shine like sapphires. He has a firm chin and sharp cheekbones. When he speaks, his voice is deep, and it sounds like he comes from the Scrubbed Desert, with its soft bur in each word. She has not been this close to a man since she fled her husband, and is blushing because she is not used to the intense and concerned stare he is giving her; she turns her face toward Tinker.

"Sorry, fair maiden—"

"She's not a maiden, I told you," Tinker interrupts.

Gwyn, glaring at Tinker, signals the man to continue with a wave of her hand.

"Anyway, my name is Larson Wingdon. I was traveling through the Shrouded Woods when that beast attacked me. So, what is it that this... little fellow put on your wound?" Larson asks, ignoring the nasty look Tinker threw at him for the insult.

"I told you, I am not little!" Tinker screams, storming over to Larson.

"Tinker, stop!" Gwyn says to him, and throwing a glare of her own at Larson, adds, "Please don't insult my friend. And it was unicorn poop. I am making a new healing potion, and my... friend," Gwyn says, turning her glare back to Tinker again, "said it would heal wounds because of the magical properties from the animal. But it didn't."

Gwyn lays back down, feeling dizzy and sick.

"That's an... interesting theory. Gross, but interesting," Larson says, pulling a chair up next to her bed.

He grabs a cloth and dips it into the basin. Holding it up to her, he asks, "May I help clean your wound? It is the least I can do for the help you gave me with the bear."

"Sure," Gwyn sighs, feeling drained and turning her head on her pillow so that the wound is facing him.

He parts her hair away from the wound and wipes the blood and poop away.

"This is a nasty wound. You might need a healer to look at it," Larson says, getting a fresh cloth and wiping more of the mess away.

"I will be fine," Gwyn says. "I just need to rest and stitch the wound if needed."

"Hey, what about this?" Tinker asks, holding up the vial of water Gwyn collected from the Crystal River. "We could see if this helps with the wound. I sense magic in it. It could help you, Gwynie."

"Sure, whatever. I don't care, so long as I can rest."

"Okay, let me pour a little on it," he says, walking over to the side of her bed.

Taking the bottle, he uncorks it and dribbles a few drops of the liquid onto the wound. Gwyn lets out a slight hiss between her teeth as if it burns her, and before Tinker's eyes, the wound closes, leaving only a red mark where it once was.

"I don't know what you did, but I felt a burning. Then the pounding in my head went away an instant later," Gwyn says, sitting up and feeling the back of her head.

"It worked, Gwynie! It healed you! How do you feel?"

"Well, Tinker, I still feel tired. But other than that, I feel fine. Maybe a little sore and stiff, but okay," Gwyn says, lying back down.

"Well, it looks like everything here is fine now, so I will return to the bear and bring its pelt and meat back," Larson says, grabbing his pack and walking out the door.

"Be careful, and stay away from any more bears," Gwyn says, throwing the soiled pillow off her bed, then rolling over and going to sleep.

Tinker hears him chuckle outside the door and snorts to himself. He would have to watch this Larson fellow. *"If Gwynie had a mate, then I need to keep this new male away from her,"* he thinks to himself, remembering she had said something about her being married, or whatever that was.

With Gwyn asleep, he makes himself busy by pouring out the old rabbit stew and cleaning the pot. Next, he finds some more of the small bottles she had used for her not-so-great potions and rinses them. Tinker then takes the ones with concoctions in them and pours them out, and rinses them as well. Finally, he takes the small vial of water from the river and sets it on the table with the rest of the bottles.

He would wait until she wakes up to ask her how she wants to go forward with the healing potion. Tinker returns to the big pot and fills it with water. Next, Tinker goes outside and, taking her pillow, cleans it and sets it out to dry overnight. Going into the little garden, he picks some vegetables growing there. Returning to the pot, he cuts the vegetables up with a knife he finds near the hearth. Putting them in the pot, he next finds some salt and garlic and puts them in there as well. Swinging the pot over the fire so it can cook, he goes over to his blanket Gwyn lets him use. Feeling satisfied, he curls up to sleep.

Chapter 6

Hours later, Gwyn wakes to the smell of something delicious cooking. She kicks the cover over her off and makes her way to the hearth. There is soup in her pot. Gwyn looks around and sees Tinker on the blanket she gave him, snoring. She grabs a bowl and pours herself some soup, then makes her way over to the table. Gwyn sees he has cleaned and set out all the vials she had, and eases them out of the way to eat the soup. It is delicious! It has a warm, robust taste to it, with the garlic added.

She finishes her bowl and gets up to get a second helping. Halfway through her second helping, she hears rustling in the corner and looks to see Tinker sitting up and rubbing his eyes. He looks around and spots Gwyn at the table. Shoving the blanket off, he walks over to her and plops down on the other chair across from her.

"How do you feel now?" he asks around an enormous yawn.

"I'm feeling better, no pain or stiffness. I was starving when I woke up, though," Gwyn says as she gets up and pours Tinker a bowl.

Handing him the steaming bowl, she pulls her own soup closer and finishes it. Feeling much better after her meal, she turns to Tinker and thinks about the water from the river. She could do so much more with water and was glad that the poop didn't work. She could put it into food or drinks and make salves and potions with it. But first, she needs to just make something to sell, then refine it once it becomes popular.

"I think we could put a cup of this water into a large pot, and with other ingredients, make a potion someone could drink or pour into their wounds. We could also add something like berries to give it a bit of flavor. What do you think, Tinker?"

"I think that is a wonderful idea. Why don't we pick some blackberries and maybe add a little steeped birch bark as well? That way, it will not only give it flavor but help relieve pain as well if any lingers. I would like to throw honey in it too."

"That could work. We can start early in the morning and work on a consumable, but also topical, potion. I think liquid would be the best way to go for our first batch. How much do you think we can get out of that small vial we have?"

"About twenty bottles if we do not go big with the glass size. Besides, we would want to keep it small, so it is easy to store."

"Perfect! It's decided then. Tomorrow, I want you to go to the village while I start the steeping process and buy us some more vials. Try to get clear ones with sturdy stoppers on the top to prevent leakage."

"Okay, Gwynie, I can do that. Just leave the coins on the table and I will get up early and get the vials. I will not take long so that I can help with the prepping process," Tinker says, yawning again.

He gets up from his chair, and carrying his bowl over to the small counter near the hearth, places it there to be washed. Turning, he goes back to his corner and curls back up to sleep. Gwyn, taking her bowl, walks over and collects Tinker's as well, and washes the two bowls, storing them on the small shelf on the other side of the hearth. Once done, Gwyn goes to her bed and reaches under it. She pulls out a small box she keeps her money in. She opens it, and pulling out a light pouch of coins, sets it on the table for Tinker in the morning. It isn't much, but it is enough to buy the glassware they need for the potions. Then she herself goes back over to her bed and falls asleep. The past two days and her run in with the bear have left her exhausted.

Dawn comes bright and early, leaving Gwyn feeling refreshed even though she only fell asleep a few hours ago. She gets up and looks towards Tinker's corner. His spot is empty, with his blanket folded. Looking at the table, she sees the money pouch is gone. She hopes Tinker would be okay getting the vials and that he doesn't get into any trouble. From the short time she has known him, he seems to have mayhem following him. She grabs a quick bite of the soup and gets dressed for the day.

    Walking to her back door, she grabs a small basket sitting to the side and goes outside to collect what she will need for the potion. She picks some rosemary and blackberries near the edge of the forest. Then goes to her small beehive that she keeps near her small flower garden near the side of the cottage. Once done collecting all her ingredients, she takes the rosemary, and with a mortar and pestle, grinds it until the aromatic oils come out. Next, she grabs her second large pot, and filling it with water, sets it over the fire in the hearth to boil. She next grabs the blackberries she collected and throws them into the pot after crushing them.

    By the time the water boils, she can smell the aroma of a forest in spring. Grabbing a spoon, she tastes the liquid. It has a sweet, woodsy taste. She then adds the water from the Crystal River to the pot. The moment the water touches the contents inside, the potion turns from a dark purple color to a vibrant, shimmering blue. Stirring the mixture to make sure all the contents of the potion are mixed, she adds the honey to it and tastes it one more time. She feels a little zing on her tongue, most likely from the river water, and a sweet taste like a berry pie.

Pulling the pot slightly off the fire so it can simmer, she goes over to the table and sits down to sort the bottles she has. She wants to let it steep for a while before she pours the potion. Maybe the longer it steeps, the better it will be, like a strong tea. Gwyn gets up, and amid grabbing herself the last of the stew, realizes it is already close to midday. Tinker has not returned yet.

Gwyn walks over to her door, ready to go find him, when he comes limping in with a small bundle squirming in his arms. Tinker has scrapes and bruises all over him. The new clothes she gave him are dirty and ripped and one of his eyes is swelling shut. He looks up at her, and smiling, sets the bundle down. The moment it hits the floor, out tumbles a small orange kitten.

"Tinker! What in all the gods' names happened to you?" Gwyn says, squatting down to get a better look at his injuries.

"Oh, this is nothing, Gwynie. I just ran into the warrior mage I tricked and he and some friends of his roughed me up a bit. Don't worry, I'm tougher than I look," he says, bending down to scoop the kitten back up into his arms.

"But you have bruises and cuts all over and they ripped your shirt. Here, sit down and let me use the new potion to heal your wounds."

"I ripped my shirt the other day to wrap your head in the forest, and I said I'm fine, so don't waste the potion on me," Tinker says, trying to wave her off.

Shaking her head, she grabs him under the arm. She leads him to the table and sits him down. Next, she goes over to the pot of simmering potion and scoops a spoonful out. She brings it over to him. She grabs the kitten with one hand while handing him the spoon so as not to spill it. Holding the little ball of fluff in her arms, she watches as Tinker first sniffs, then drinks the spoonful of potion. They both wait for a moment as his bruises fade and his scrapes close.

Hugging the kitten to her chest, she smiles at him. Excitedly, she asks, "So, what do you think of the potion?"

"I think it is great, Gwynie. It tastes great, and the healing process was fast. I think we are on to something!" he says just as brightly, jumping off the chair and taking the kitten from her.

"Now we must help him!"

"I was just getting ready to ask you about the kitten. Where did you find him?"

"I found him after those men attacked me. He was behind a water barrel near the glass shop. I grabbed him and brought him back here. He seems to have a hurt paw. Can you help him?"

"Ah yes, those men. I will have to give that warrior mage a piece of my mind. I don't like confrontation, but I don't like it when my friends get hurt either. As for the kitten, yes, I think if we slip a little of the potion in some milk, it should heal his paw," Gwyn says, grabbing the little limb to inspect it.

The injury on the paw looks as if something caught it, but they can find no other damage. Taking a little of the potion, Gwyn puts a few drops into some milk she has stored in her ice box outside. She sets the little saucer of milk down on the floor. Tinker sets the kitten down, and he limps to the saucer and laps up the milk. He acts like he has had no food for a while. Once the kitten has finished his milk, he toddles back over to Tinker and weaves between his legs, limp gone.

That is when Gwyn gets a good look at it. It has fuzzy orange fur with a long, puffy tail; it looks to be about two months old, with ridiculously long whiskers. But something about the way the fur lies on the kitten's back doesn't seem right. She walks over to it and places her hand on the fur of his back, petting the fur the wrong way. As she does so, small quills the same color as the fur stand up with the fur and Gwyn pulls her hand back, startled.

"No! This can't be possible!" she thinks to herself as she grabs the tail and parts the fur on the tip to reveal a scorpion-like stinger on the tip.

"It is! The kitten is a miniature manticore," Gwyn says, looking now at Tinker. "Where did you find him again?"

"Near the glass maker, where I got your bottles. He was behind a barrel, limping around, looking for food."

"It is illegal to have or breed mini-manticores because they can be so unpredictable. But I heard the underground market has them for the more unsavory people," Gwyn says, scratching the manticore's head.

"Can we keep him? I want to call him Cuddles."

"Yes, we can keep him. We will have to be careful about it, though. We will have to make sure no one finds out he is a manticore, or they will take him away."

It would be easy enough to keep Cuddles hidden if no one ruffles his fur the wrong way. He doesn't have the human-like face a normal manticore would have, as well as being smaller and more catlike than lion-like. The tail would have to be watched, though, so the barb would poison no one. But that opens a new possibility for Gwyn. She can milk the stinger of the poison and sell it to travelers as a self-defense potion of sorts to put on their arrow tips to help take down monsters. She will have to wait, though. Because of how young Cuddles is, she will have to wait for him to mature so the poison would be more potent.

"Can I see the bottles you bought so that I can fill them and get ready for our first sale? I think our first day we should give a few out for free so that it gets out there and circulating to draw customers in."

"Sure, here they are, Gwynie. I got about twenty of them. I think one or two might have gotten crushed though. Sorry," he says, handing her the small bag of glass bottles.

"It's fine. It's not your fault they broke, and we can get more once we sell them and start making a profit."

They spend the next hour filling the potion bottles with the healing potion she made. They fill about thirty of the bottles with a little left over for another batch later. Next, she and Tinker repair the broken table, so they have something to display the potions and get ready for bed. Gwyn can't help but feel excited. She is going to sell something and start her business. She can't wait for dawn to come so she can set up. The perfect place is where she is. She will set her table up at the bounty job board where, when questors pick up jobs, they can also pick up one of her potions. Feeling too excited to sleep, she tosses and turns for a bit before she drifts off.

Chapter 7

Dawn comes, and Gwyn awakes with a warm, fuzzy ball curled next to her neck. In the night, Cuddles must have slipped into the bed with her. She smiles at the little manticore and scratches him behind the ear. Getting up, she gets dressed for the day and packs all the potions into her pack, and eats a quick bite of bread and cheese. As she is eating, Tinker awakes and gets himself ready for the day. He is a little stiff in his movements, and Gwyn decides when they come back for the night, she will make him a bed so he can be comfortable.

The stiffness cannot erase the smile from his face, though, as he eats his small breakfast. He is feeling the excitement as well. They both have high hopes for their potion, and nothing can dampen their spirits about it. With one final check, making sure they have everything, and Tinker setting a bowl of milk and some scraps of rabbit meat down for Cuddles, they leave for the village. As they walk, Tinker is skipping toward the village. It is like him getting beaten up yesterday never happened. Gwyn wishes she could be more like that, and forget the pain and embrace the day like him. Maybe with more time, she will.

When they reach the board, Gwyn sets her little table up and starts setting out her potions. She doesn't set them all out this time, learning from the first time she met Tinker. As she is setting the potions out, Tinker reads the board. She walks over and reads the board as well. One poster describes a missing woman of about five feet, with wavy, chocolate-brown hair and blue eyes. Feeling her pulse quickening, she rips the poster down and stuffs it into the pack with the remaining potions.

"That poster sounded like it was describing you, Gwynie," Tinker says, giving her a puzzled look.

"No, don't be silly, it's not me. Here, help me finish setting up the table before the village wakes up for the day," Gwyn says, changing the subject.

With one last look at her, Tinker arranges the final potions on the table and sits behind the table so as not to block the view. Gwyn comes around and stands beside him, feeling anxious. Will she have to move again? She doesn't think he would look for her this far. But if word gets out that she is here, then he might come for her. If she has to leave, she will. She has little to her name anyway, so she will be able to just leave. As terrifying as that thought is, she has to at least make some money before she leaves so she can buy supplies and food.

While she worries, Tinker sits on the ground practicing turning a rock into a flower and changing it back. A shadow falls over him from behind.

"I thought I told you to never show your disgusting frog face here again?" the warrior mage snarls down at Tinker.

"Last I checked, you didn't own this village, and I can go wherever I want," Tinker snaps back.

He stands as tall as he can, puffing his chest out. Trying to look bigger in front of the warrior mage.

"I guess we will have to teach you a lesson that will last," the warrior mage says. Looking over his shoulder, he gives a sharp whistle.

Three large men come walking around the corner of the tavern near the board and amble over to where the table is set up. They first leer at Gwyn, then turn to Tinker, cracking their knuckles. At first Gwyn is terrified. They outnumber them four to two, and the situation is not in their favor. But she cannot let them hurt Tinker again. So, she steps up with a newfound courage.

"Why don't you guys leave us alone? We are doing nothing wrong and are minding our own business. You are the ones harassing us," Gwyn says, standing tall and clenching her shaking hands into fists to try to not give away the fact that she is terrified.

"Oh ho, look at this, boys! The little mouse thinks she's brave." The warrior mage laughs as he turns his attention toward Gwyn.

That is when he notices the glove on her hand with the stone bulging underneath it.

"What is this you have in your glove?" he says, snatching her arm roughly and ripping the glove off her hand.

"Hey, leave her alone!" Tinker shouts, trying to push the man away from Gwyn.

But the man just shoves Tinker away toward the other men, who grab him and pin him to the ground. As Tinker struggles against the men, the warrior mage dumps the aiming stone out of the glove and watches it hit the ground. The man stares at it for a moment, then he tightens his grip on Gwyn's arm. He looks her straight in the eye and slaps her. The hit is so hard she staggers back, and if it wasn't for him gripping her arm, she would have fallen to the ground.

"So, you are in on it, too. You are a thieving bitch just like him! You tried to act innocent when this scum first took it, but it looks like you were just playing an act to get my stone. " he says, pulling his arm back for another slap.

"No, I swear that was the first time I had ever met any of

you!" Gwyn says, raising her other hand to protect her face while trying to explain. But she cannot say any more when she is slapped across the face again, harder, this time splitting her lip.

"Stop it! Stop hitting her! She had nothing to do with your stone. It was me! I took it! Please stop hitting her!" Tinker begs on the ground.

"Oh, don't worry, your turn is coming next. But first, this bitch has to learn her lesson about stealing from others," he says as he slaps her again, this time knocking her to the ground.

The other men holding Tinker just laugh as the man keeps hitting Gwyn. Tinker struggles against his captors, to no avail. All Gwyn can do is hold her hands over her face to protect herself from the severe blows raining down on her.

"I think that's quite enough!" A loud booming voice comes from behind them.

The warrior mage turns to see Larson striding over toward them with a look of absolute rage on his face. There are large bundles hanging from his belt and he has a white furry bundle strapped to his back. He has just come back from taking care of the bear Gwyn had slain. He looks down at Gwyn, scanning her from head to toe before, he turns his full attention to the man that was hitting her.

"So, Duncan, what is this? It's the first time I see you in months, and I find you beating not just a woman, but my friend," Larson says, glaring at Duncan still crouched over Gwyn.

"And why do you have my little goblin friend pinned down as well?" he demands, turning to look at the men holding Tinker.

"This woman and her goblin scum have stolen my stone. So I am teaching them the consciences of their actions," Duncan says, straightening and turning toward Larson. "They have stolen the stone you made for me and then tried to pass cat shit off as it when I demanded it back."

As he says this, Tinker snickers to himself, and one man holding him down punches him in the gut, making him curl up in a ball. Larson looks to the men, then at Tinker and with a sigh reaches into one of his packs hanging from his belt. He pulls out a red stone that looks just like the one that had fallen to the ground and hands it to Duncan. Next, he scoops up the other stone, and reaching out to Gwyn, helps her to her feet and puts the stone in her hands. He plucks a potion bottle off the table and shoves it into Duncan's chest.

Gruffly, he says, "This should be payment enough for the lost stone. If she didn't have the stone when we met in the woods, then I would not be standing here talking to you today. She used the stone to slay a mist bear with just a spear and I think letting her keep the stone is payment enough for my life debt."

"This little mouse slew a mist bear? Impossible! It takes at least three expert hunters to fell one."

"True, but if you do not believe me, here is the pelt of the beast she has slain. Skinned and ready to be tanned and made into a cloak," Larson says, pointing to the furry bundle on his back. "Now, away with you all. My companions and I have work to do. I hope to never catch you hitting a woman in my presence again, or I will do more than just speak up."

The men, looking to Duncan, let Tinker go when he gives them a nod, and the four of them slink away into the tavern.

"Thank you for stepping in," Gwyn says, wiping the blood from her mouth.

"It was the least I could do, and I am sorry I was not here sooner to prevent your injuries. Are you all right? Your nose is bleeding," he says, reaching over to wipe the blood off her face.

As he reaches for her, she flinches away and wipes the blood from her face with the sleeve of her tunic, not looking him in the eye.

"I'm fine. Just roughed up a little, nothing that my new potion can't fix," she says, grabbing one potion off the table and taking a sip.

Larson, kicking himself for startling her after such an incident, watches her fresh bruises and split lip heal right before his eyes. It astonishes him that the healing potion works. Most potions take at the very least an hour to work. But this potion has worked in an instant, even better than his enchanted stones for healing. The gouge on his leg from the bear is now just healed after two days. He picks up another of the potion bottles and inspects it.

"This is amazing! You made this with what you brought from the forest?"

"Well, the water, not the poop, but yes," Gwyn says, blushing. "I had wanted to study alchemy when I was younger, so I asked my father to buy me a book for beginners. I began studying the book until my mother found out and put a stop to it, claiming that a young lady of my station should only need to worry about finding a husband and not foolish hobbies like alchemy. Since I was little, I wanted to open a shop of my own. But to sell potions and items for questors, and not wine like my father."

"What family do you hail from, if you don't mind me asking?" Larson inquires.

Gwyn hesitates for a moment before she replies. "I am the daughter of a very prominent wine merchant. My father owns and runs the Bix vineyards, where he makes and sells the best and most well-known wine in Sehill."

She is still somewhat hesitant about sharing too much of her past, especially if posters of her have appeared around the outer villages of the country now. She doesn't want her husband to find her or the wrong person to overhear her and tell her husband where she was at for a bit of gold.

Larson, looking at her with a wide smile, exclaims, "Well, I'm impressed! Not only are you a fine potion maker, but come from the family who makes my favorite wine! I have to say, once people learn of this potion, you will have a hard time keeping up with demand. Can I partner with you to sell my staves and enchanted stones along with your potion?"

"I would have to think about it and discuss it with Tinker, but I do not see why not. The more products we have, the better we can make a sale. But for today, we are just giving away free samples so that people can learn about it and will want to come back to buy more. They say word of mouth is the best advertisement," Gwyn says with a chuckle.

They spend the rest of the morning and most of the day handing out Gwyn's potions, and well past lunchtime, head back to Gwyn's cottage. When they reach the cottage, Gwyn lets them in as she sets the table outside and closes the door behind everyone. An ecstatic Cuddles, who goes straight to Tinker and starts purring as he winds around his legs, greets them. Placing the bag on the table, Gwyn pulls the leftover potions out. As she is doing it, the missing poster flutters toward the floor. Larson, who is also setting his bundles on the table, stoops to pick up the paper.

"What is this?" he asks, showing the paper to Gwyn. "This looks like you."

Snatching the paper out of his hand and throwing it into the fire, Gwyn just smiles and says, "It's no one, just a paper I saw on the ground and picked up. That girl looks nothing like me.

Now, what is in the bundles you have brought?"

Larson looks at her for a moment, then turns to Tinker, who just shrugs and starts playing with Cuddles. He turns back to Gwyn, deciding to drop the subject for now and pointing at the white bundle first.

"This is the pelt of the bear you killed. I brought it for you, and if you would allow it, I can set it up to dry so you can make a cloak out of it. The other bundles are meat from the bear that we can eat or trade. The decision is up to you," Larson says, patting each bundle as he spoke about them.

"That would be wonderful, and it is just big enough. I could take some to make a shawl for Tinker as well for the winter. As for the meat, we can eat some and sell the rest tomorrow. Bear meat is not my favorite."

"I can make dinner. How about vegetable soup again?" Tinker says, standing up from where he and Cuddles are playing and dusting himself off.

"While both of you are busy working on your tasks, I will make you a more permanent and comfortable bed, Tinker," Gwyn says, pulling her sewing kit out.

They work throughout the rest of the day, Tinker making dinner, Larson stretching the hide, and Gwyn sewing. By the end of the evening, the cottage has a delicious smell in it and Gwyn is just shaking out the bed she has made Tinker. It is just two old sheets sewn together that she has stuffed with cotton, along with long grasses and hay growing outside. She puts it in his corner, takes his blanket, and spreads it over the top of it. Larson comes in a little later, wiping his hands and smiling at Tinker.

"Your soup smells amazing! What did you put in it?"

"I used tomatoes and carrots this time with some garlic,

basil, thyme, and salt. It should be ready to eat now."

"Both you boys wash up while I serve the soup, and then we can talk more about our partnership," Gwyn says, stretching.

She goes over to the bowls she has and spoons into each a generous helping of the soup. Next, she grabs the last of her bread and sets it on the table with the soup bowls. She grabs three cups and fills them each with fresh water. By the time she is done, Tinker and Larson have come over to the table, and they sit and eat. As they eat, they discuss the partnership they will have and agree that if either of them sold anything, then they would give the other ten percent of the earnings.

Upon agreeing to the terms, they write it down, and each signs their name on it. After the agreement, and they had eaten their fill, they all go to bed, with Larson insisting he will sleep outside and then find better sleeping arrangements in the morning. Tired as she is, Gwyn cannot help but smile at how productive her day has been. She has made a potion that worked, stood up to some bullies, and she has given out some of her potion. But the most surprising of all is having made a partnership with Larson. She never thought she would ever get close to a man again. Everything is looking up for her. But then she thinks about the missing poster and as she drifts off to sleep, her worries trouble her throughout the night.

Chapter 8

The chains hanging from the ceiling clink together as Gwyn sways just inches above the floor. She is in the wine cellar again. For what crime she has done now, she does not know. All she knows is she is going to be in for a long, painful night. It is not the first time she has hung from these chains. But if she is lucky, it will be her last if he goes too far and kills her.

The first time her husband hung her up, she wore the wrong shoes with her dress to a banquet he hosted. It had embarrassed him for her to dress in front of prominent guests, he had told her, and he did not like being embarrassed. That beating for something so trivial was the first time she had ever been hit in her life. Her parents always made her sit in a corner whenever she got into trouble. He had taken a crop to her that time.

But this time, it looks like he will use something more severe. He has been favoring the nine tails more of late and her back shows the proof of it. She can feel him behind her, readying for the first strike. As she swings from the chains, she withdraws into herself and lets her mind go free.

"This is for your own good, dear. You must learn to be a good wife and obey my every word. But it seems you just cannot learn this lesson. No matter, I am a very patient man, and you will learn this lesson with time. Even if it kills you to do so," her husband says, running his hand down her back.

She hears him step back and get into position, and then she feels the ripping pain of the first strike.

Gwyn wakes up with a gasp. It has been a while since she has had a nightmare about her married life. One of pain, misery, and humiliation. A life she was lucky enough to survive and escape from, and one she vowed to never return to.

Sitting up, she wipes the cold sweat off her face and glances around. It looks like she hasn't woken Tinker up. She lays back down but has difficulty falling asleep again. When she does, it is a dreamless sleep.

Over the next few weeks, Tinker and Gwyn settle into a quick routine. One makes breakfast while the other packs and gets ready for the day. They either go to the Crystal River and collect more water or go to Lancegate to sell potions. After that day of giving out free samples, word got around, and questors started showing up to buy her potion. Larson was selling his enchanted stones as well, and they made a steady profit.

Gwyn now has enough saved up to purchase a horse, which she has been longing to buy for a while, so it would be easier and faster to travel to and from the river. It will also be great in the future for when she wants to set out for Inaslas and set up a more permanent shop. But she will need more money before she can move there, and to make more money, she needs a new potion.

So, one day, she posts a wanted sign on the bulletin. The post said, "Wanted: one horse for travel and farm work. Willing to pay fifty gold coins. Please inquire in the Drunken Dragon."

The Drunken Dragon is the name of the tavern in the village and a major meet up spot for questors to conduct their business. Gwyn checks the tavern every day after posting on the board with no luck. But she has faith that since it was the end of fall, someone will sell her a horse for money to feed their family during the winter. With any luck, the horse will have a sound foot and mild temper. But Gwyn will take almost anything now so that when she travels to the river in the winter, she will not get trapped in the woods by the snow.

On the last day of fall, as she is packing up for the day, she makes her way toward the Tavern.

"Tinker, I am going to check and see if anyone has answered my post. You go on ahead and start dinner for us. Larson will come over tonight from the Inn, so make enough for him as well."

"Do I have to, Gwynie? I dislike that big oaf," Tinker says, making an annoyed face.

"Yes, now go on. I don't understand why you don't like him when he has been nothing but nice to us and is our business partner." Gwyn says, dismissing him and turning toward the Drunken Dragon.

"Okay, Gwynie. If you say so," Tinker says with a huff as he makes his way to the cottage.

Gwyn walks through the front door and up to the bar. The golden-haired woman is working at the tavern tonight. Joslyn is her name. She took Gwyn under her wing and would sometimes sneak Gwyn some extra day-old bread and cheese when she first arrived at the village. She is wiping up a spill when Gwyn comes up to the bar and sits down on a stool.

"Before you ask, yes, someone has answered your post about a horse. The man said he would be back in about an hour to talk with you," Joslyn says, sliding Gwyn a glass of cider.

"Wonderful, I will sit and wait then. Tell me, what does this man look like so I can recognize him when he walks in?" Gwyn responds, taking a sip.

"Well, he is short with a hunched back, I would say around fifty years old at the least. He has long, gray hair braided with a squall's feather tied to it," Joslyn says, continuing to wipe down the bar.

"Should be easy enough to spot. Tell me, how you have been?"

The two women talk for a while as Gwyn drinks her cider. Close to dark, an older man walks in and comes up to the bar. He looks just as Joslyn described, right down to the feather in his hair. He sits down next to Gwyn and orders himself some ale. Taking a long drag of his drink, he looks at Gwyn with a squint.

"You must be the girl wanting a horse," he says, taking another long drink. "Now the one I want to sell is long in the tooth but is a hard worker. Solid body, with sturdy legs. Just eats too much for me to keep up with him anymore."

"I don't mind an older horse, sir, as long as he can get me from one place to another," Gwyn says with a smile. "Did you bring him with you?"

"Aye girly, he is just outside tided to a post. Now listen here, he can be stubborn sometimes, but he isn't mean-natured. I think he will fit your needs."

"Excellent. I will go look at him now. What's his name?"

"Dawn Star is his name and go on out and look at him. See if you like him. I'll meet you after I finish my drink," the old man says, turning back to his half-finished ale.

Gwyn, excited to see her new horse, jumps off her stool and rushes outside. She looks around and sees a large, dappled gray draft horse standing next to a post. She approaches the horse, and when she calls out the horse's name, he turns his head and pricks his ears toward her.

"Well, aren't you a handsome boy?" Gwyn says while reaching out and stroking his soft nose.

"What do you think?" comes the voice of the old man. "Does

he suit you?"

"Yes, he is perfect. I will take him," Gwyn says, reaching into her side pouch hanging on her belt and handing the old man the payment.

The old man takes the payment, and with a final pat to the horse's neck, turns and walks away into the deepening night. Gwyn takes the lead tied to the post and walks the horse home. When she reaches the cottage, she walks Dawn Star around back to a fenced area Larson has put up for her. She takes the bridle off Dawn Star and turns him loose, letting him explore his new paddock. He sniffs and paws at the ground. Finding a spot he is satisfied with, he lays down with a groan and rolls over. Chuckling, Gwyn turns from watching him roll and leaves him to get settled for the night. She checks to make sure he has plenty of water for the night, then heads in herself. When she walks in, Tinker collides with her with an excited smile on his face.

"I heard hoof steps. Did you get a horse?" Tinker asks, trying to peer around her through the back door.

"Yes, I did, but let him settle for the night and you can see him tomorrow. What did you make for dinner tonight?"

"He made fish stew with parsnips in it," Larson says, sitting next to the hearth.

"Ah, you made it. How was your day?" Gwyn asks, walking over to him and giving him a quick hug.

They have gotten closer over the past few weeks. Small touches here and there, catching the other staring. Little things that make Gwyn think Larson might want more than friendship. He is very attractive, with his dark red hair and blue eyes. But she is terrified of what might happen, especially with how her marriage went. Her husband, too, seemed nice in the beginning, but became a monster behind closed doors. Gwyn just isn't quite ready to let someone in, even though she feels comfortable with Larson now.

"It was rather good. I slipped into the woods and collected more water for you from the river. Also, I picked up the bearskin. I had the tanner make a cloak for you and there was some left over to make a small shawl," Larson says, handing over a large, wrapped parcel. He next gives Tinker a similar one, but much smaller. "The fur turned out excellent, and it should keep you both warm this winter."

"Thank you so much, Larson. It's beautiful!" Gwyn says, unwrapping it and throwing the cloak over her shoulders. A small chain clasp keeps it in place. "What do you think, Tinker?"

Tinker smiles up at her as he wraps his shawl around his neck.

"It looks great, Gwynie! 'Gwynie the Bear Slayer' is what I should call you now."

"No, don't you dare! It was pure luck I killed the bear. But thank you, anyway. Your shawl looks fantastic."

"Yes, thank you so much, oaf, for making this for me," Tinker says, taking it off and putting it in his corner by his bed.

Larson just smiles and shakes his head. They know when Tinker decides on a certain name for someone, he never changes it. They all sit around the table and eat their supper, each talking about their own day. After eating, Larson and Tinker clean up while Gwyn makes a fresh batch of healing potions and sets them aside for sale. They sit around the fire, just enjoying each other's company, when Larson speaks up.

"Have you ever thought about using a weapon for defense? I could teach you how if you would like. I just figured since in spring we will move to Inaslas, you would want to learn how to defend yourself."

"That's a great idea," Tinker says. "I would like to use a dagger."

"It would be good to learn, and it would help if we need to defend our future shop from ruffians and thieves," Gwyn says, turning to Larson. "When would you like to train?"

"I could start coming by every morning before you go to Lancegate, and we could train for about an hour. Does that sound good?"

"I think that would be fine. What about you, Tinker?"

"Yup, sounds good to me. I can't wait to get my very own dagger."

"That's what I will do. I will train you both with a dagger first, then I will train you with a bow and a small sword that fits your size, Gwyn. We can start as soon as I get some daggers, a short sword, and a bow. It should take me about two days to get everything."

"Well, it's settled. Then we will see you in two days' time and begin our training," Gwyn says, yawning.

"Well, I'll be off then. See you in two days," Larson says, getting up and walking toward the door.

Gwyn gets up and walks him out. Stepping outside with him into the night, she gives him one more hug and says farewell. Larson stands in front of her for a moment, just staring at her. He looks like he wants to say something, but turns, and with a farewell, walks away into the night. Gwyn feels her face heat, wondering what he might have wanted to stay. Could she allow herself to let him get closer? Could she move on from her past and open up to others again? Time will tell if she has healed enough to start a new chapter with someone else. Maybe one day she can tell both Larson and Tinker about her past, her whole past, with all the horrors that come with it, and not just say she was once married. But would they pity her then and think differently of her once they know? She doesn't know, and is terrified to find out, because she doesn't want what she has now to change for the worse if they do.

Chapter 9

The two days pass by, with Gwyn and Tinker going to the village to sell potions. On the day of Larson's return, they decide not to go to the village and opt to stay in and relax. Business has been slowing down and Gwyn gets to thinking that maybe it is time to create a new potion or two to sell along with her healing potion. But what can she do? She and Tinker talk at length, and neither come up with an idea for a new portion that is just as good as the first one. Then, on the day that Larson is due to come back, Gwyn gets an idea. What if they could make a potion that would give them extra speed for a short amount of time? One that could help someone flee in a sticky situation, or boost their movements in a battle.

    What could they use for the ingredients, though? Gwyn grabs her old alchemy book off her nightstand and starts flipping through the pages. She finds a potion that sparked her interest: an agility potion. The key ingredient is a quick seed. A quick seed is a type of berry that grows from a very scraggly bush in the cold, dry climate of the Scrubbed Desert off to the south. The seeds are easy to buy because once you plant one seed, it grows like a weed outside of its natural barren climate. Gwyn has the bush in her back garden. The problem is she needs to make something stronger that would last longer and have more control than the seed. The potion in the alchemy book says it gives the user speed for thirty seconds, but you would lose motor control of your body. She needs an ingredient that would give her potion not just speed but motor control while using it.

Just as she is pondering the recipe, an idea strikes her. Why not use the feathers of a squall? A squall is one of the fastest birds in the country and has precise motor skills. They can hoover in the air, fly backwards, and even fly upside down while keeping their speed. Gwyn could take some feathers and burn them, then add the ashes to the potion recipe. It would increase the control and add an extra boost to the quick seeds.

They will have to travel to the coast where the squalls dwell. But since it is becoming winter, she will have to wait till spring when they preen all the old feathers off and grow new feathers for the mating season. The third option is to make a paralyzing potion using Cuddles' venom from his tail. Gwyn has already found out the hard way that his tail barb contains a venom that causes paralysis when she stepped on his tail and lost all feeling in her leg for about half the day. It would be so easy to make. All she has to do is milk his tail barb and then add a few other ingredients to it so that customers could just dip their weapons in it. She would have to get Tinker to help her.

It is perfect. They can leave her cottage and go to the coast. It is one hundred miles from the village. But first she will need to ask Larson and Tinker what they think of her way to improve and create a better agility potion. She will wait till tonight to talk to them. She knows Tinker would be excited, but since Larson is her partner now, she has to make sure he agrees as well.

As the day goes on, she brings the subject of the paralysis salve to Tinker.

"Do you think you could help me milk Cuddles' barb so I can extract the venom out of it? I would like to make a salve out of it to sell."

"Sure, Gwynie, I can help you. What else were you thinking

of putting in it?"

"The dried petals of a petrified blossom. It will help with the salve's potency, along with melted beeswax so that when it hardens, could be rubbed onto weapons."

"That sounds perfect, Gwynie!" Tinker exclaims. "We can also keep it in liquid form for us to keep for emergencies. Stopping us from getting hurt again by people bigger and stronger than us will be our new top priority. Feeling helpless while that man was hitting you was not a good feeling."

"I feel the same way, Tinker. I was once helpless, and I vowed to never be again."

"How were you helpless?"

Gwyn looks at Tinker and says with a sigh, "Remember when I told you I was married? Well, I am no longer with him because he was very cruel to me. He would starve me and lock me in my room, but the worst was he used to chain me up and then beat me. He would do it for the smallest of reasons, too. If I was not wearing the proper shoes, or I spoke out of turn when he had guests over. He would hang me from the ceiling on chains, and then he would whip me for hours. And when he was done, sometimes he would just leave me to hang for the rest of the night. Other times, I would be bound on my knees with my hands pulled behind my back between my ankles, and a collar and rope pulled back between them as well. If he tied me up like that, he wouldn't beat me. He would just let me sit like that, trapped in that horrible position until he deemed it time to let me loose. If he wasn't punishing me, he was forcing himself on me, saying it was his right as a husband. He took whatever he wanted whenever he wanted from me and there was nothing I could do to stop him."

Gwyn turns away from Tinker as she feels tears falling down

her face. She has been holding on to what happened to her for so long that even as she tells him, she is letting all her emotions she has been holding back out as well. She couldn't trust anyone with her story for fear of once they found out who she was married to, they would send her back to him. It feels good to tell Tinker what happened to her. She knows she can trust him. As she is crying, she feels small arms wrapping around her and squeezing her. She looks to see Tinker hugging her.

She hugs him back as she continues.

"It wasn't just physical. He would degrade me in front of others. Told me I was worthless, did nothing right, and would never amount to anything. He took my money away from me where I had nothing and was nothing. I was one-hundred percent reliant on him for everything. He even had the staff at the house monitor me and report my every mistake to him. I just couldn't take it anymore, so one night while he slept, I fled. I packed a small bag and left in the night, never looking back. It has been over a year now, and he is still looking for me. That poster you saw me rip down and burn? It was me, Tinker! It was me! I must always look over my shoulders. Never stopping long enough to feel safe."

"Well, you are safe now, Gwyneth. I will never let him harm you. We are friends and friends protect each other. You had to be so strong by yourself, but now you have me. I will protect you and Cuddles, too."

With a sniffling laugh, Gwyn hugs Tinker back and then strokes Cuddles on his head when he jumps up on the bed with them.

"I have been so broken; I am unbreakable now."

"We will be unbreakable together. Now let us prepare for our first fighting lesson. He should arrive soon, and we must get ready. First, let me milk the venom out of Cuddles' tail, so we have it for the salve."

"I'll make dinner then for after our lesson." Gwyn sniffles as she gets off the bed and starts prepping dinner.

As Gwyn makes dinner, Tinker goes over to the shelf where they keep the bottles for their potion and selects a small, green, orb-shaped one. When he first purchased the bottle at the glass maker, he saw it and had to have it. He has been saving it for a special potion and now is the time to use it. He walks over to Cuddles and starts stroking him from the base of his neck to the base of his tail. It will be easier to extract the venom if Cuddles is relaxed. Stroking up his tail, Tinker parts the fur at the tip and presses the barb tip on the top of the bottle. A milky, clear venom comes trickling out and into the jar. Tinker has collected about a teaspoon of the venom when Cuddles gets up and prances away to his food bowl, which Gwyn has filled with cut meats. Tinker holds the bottle up to the light to examine the venom inside. It will take several more attempts before they have enough to make the paralysis salve, but it is a great start, and the darker bottle will help protect the venom inside from any light.

Tinker sets the bottle down near his bed and walks over to help set the table for dinner. They are finishing dinner and cleaning up when they hear a knock at the door. Gwyn walks over to the door to answer it as Tinker sets all the dishes away for washing them. Opening the door, she lets Larson in from outside. With a smile, she asks him how his trip was.

"It was rather uneventful. There were some weird rumors floating around, though, of dead or sick-looking animals walking around. Some churches claimed to have had graves robbed of the actual corpses," he said, shrugging off his long wool cloak. "I heard good feedback about your potion. Healers are using it for some of their treatments now."

"That's great about the potions!" Gwyn exclaims. "We might partner up with some healers in Inaslas and supply them with our healing potion and maybe come up with some other potions they could use for their work. I hope the rumors are false, though. Why would anyone want to steal someone's corpse?"

"I do not know. But I brought a dagger for each of you, and we can train in the morning. First, though, we must train our bodies before we can train with a blade. I have a routine set up for you both to start right away."

"What kind of routine?" Tinker asks, looking nervous.

"Well, in the morning, you will each run a mile to warm up. After that, you will both train your arms by doing fifty pushups to strengthen your arms. Next, you will do fifty sit-ups so that we can work on your core strength. A weak core makes a weak fighter. You will do fifty squats to strengthen your legs for a firm base. Everything strengthens your body so that when you use the blade, you have the balance and strength behind it. The weapon is only as good as the person who wields it."

As Larson is speaking, Tinker's eyes get bigger and bigger.

"How do you expect us to do all that on the first day?" he exclaims.

"It will be hard in the beginning, but with time, you will increase your numbers in your routine, and it will become easier for you to do each task. I have full confidence in you both that you will have no problem with this. After the workout, we will run through some self-defense moves. Once you become comfortable with them, we will add the dagger. Also, Gwyn, I want to teach you the bow."

"Whatever you will teach us, I will be grateful to learn," Gwyn says with a sigh.

Just like Tinker, she feels overwhelmed with all the training she will have to do just to hold a dagger.

"Now the daggers I got are dull-tipped for practicing. What I am giving you for you to keep for protection is being made and will be ready after winter. I had them made from the bronze claws of the mist bear," Larson says, handing them both a practice dagger. "The daggers I commissioned are in Inaslas, being made by one of the finest blacksmiths."

"That's good news to hear, because I was thinking this spring we should move to Inaslas and make our shop more permanent. I even thought of some new potions I want to run by you. Also, I came up with a name I was thinking of calling the shop," Gwyn says, while placing the dagger on her nightstand and picking up her alchemy book.

"The first potion I want to make is an agility potion. I saw a recipe in my book for agility. But the problem with it is that it leaves the user unstable and sacrifices dexterity. So, I was thinking of using the feathers from a squall, one of the fastest and most agile birds in the world. It would be so easy to get feathers this spring during their mating season. Feathers will be everywhere from the preening. We could leave for the coast, collect some feathers, and then turn around and go straight to Inaslas. What do you think?"

"That sounds like a good idea. How would the squall feather help the potion?" Larson asks, flipping through the book she handed him.

"Well, it would add control to the user. Instead of just pure speed, it will also help with controlled movement and accuracy." Gwyn explains, turning to the page and showing him the recipe.

"Okay, and what about the next potion? And what name have you thought up for the shop?"

"Well, I was thinking of making a salve with paralyzing qualities in it to rub onto weapons. I would use the venom of some creature and the petals from a petrified blossom. It would be a more nonlethal way to take someone down and not kill them. The name I want to use for the shop is Questor's Emporium."

"I love the name! Now that second salve sounds great. Could you also make it into a drinkable potion as well?" Larson says, smiling and rubbing his hands together.

He is getting excited that they are going to expand their line of products and that they now have a name for their business. It would become easier for people to request their products with the shop soon to be established in Inaslas. They could have a much bigger clientele than just questors. Also, with the new ideas he has for his stone enchantments, he is sure he can contribute more.

"I have a few ideas myself for stone enchantments. I am going to create a locator charm for a loved one to wear so that they can always be found, as well as a bracer that can enhance the magic of the user. Do you have any suggestions for an enchantment?"

"I like the idea of locator charms. You could make one for each of us to wear. We would have two on a necklace with each locating each other. For example, my two would be for you and Tinker. As for other suggestions, why not try to create something for stealth? Something to hide one's sound or movements," Gwyn says, tapping a finger to her lips as she thinks.

Larson loves seeing how she thinks up ideas and solves problems. She is not only beautiful, with her long, dark, chocolate hair and smooth, fair skin, but she is smart, too. He feels drawn to her. It is as if her ocean-blue eyes are pulling him in. He hopes to get closer to her, but she always seems to keep herself at arm's length. It is better than when they first met, when she would shrink away or flinch at a sudden movement he made. She tries to hide it, but sometimes, when she thinks he isn't paying attention, she withdraws into herself. Maybe with the training routine, he can become closer and learn more about her. He has a few questions he wants to ask her about her past, but feels they need to be closer first. And he still wonders about that poster that she burned. Was that not her on the poster, or is she hiding something from him? With his inner thoughts turning toward places they didn't need to go, he gets up and stretches.

"Well, I will make my way to the inn and get some rest. I recommend you both do the same. I will be here an hour before the sun comes up to start our training, so make sure you have rested and eat a light breakfast to not get sick during the training." As he speaks, he walks to the door and lets himself out.

Once he leaves, Gwyn and Tinker both do as he says and get ready for bed. Gwyn feels excited about their training to start, but Tinker is anxious about the training. He knows he is not in the best of shape. He has gained weight back from being exiled from his clan, and he just hopes that he can keep up and not make a fool of himself. In the morning, he will have to wait and see.

Dawn comes, and they both do as Larson said, having a small breakfast of toast and water. They step outside and wait for Larson to show up. They don't have to wait long before they see him jogging toward them in the crisp morning air. As he stops in front of them, he keeps jogging in place as he speaks.

"Okay, so first you have to stretch and warm your body up so you do not pull any of your muscles. Here, I will show you."

He stops jogging long enough to show them a series of quick stretches they can perform, and once they are done, he has them follow him in a brisk jog. They jog down the road for a while and when they reach about halfway, both Tinker and Gwyn are panting and sweating. By the time they turn around and reach Gwyn's house again, they are both gasping for air. Tinker flops down on the ground and is struggling to catch his breath.

"Come on, guys, that was just the warmup. The real fun is about to start. Now in a push-up position like this," Larson says through pants as he drops to the ground, ready to do push-ups.

Gwyn and Tinker glance at each other, then both get into position. Once they are ready, Larson has them start, with Gwyn counting each lift out loud. Once they have completed their push-ups, Larson has them do sit-ups and squats. When they finish, they are both laying on the ground, unable to move.

"I hate you!" Tinker pants as he glares at Larson.

Larson just smiles at him, and while wiping the sweat off his brow, says, "You may hate me now, but you will thank me later."

"I doubt that," Tinker puffs at him.

"Okay! Break time is over. While your bodies are still loose, I will show you some basic footwork to try. We will just work on footwork today, and tomorrow after that, I will add hand blocks and strikes. Once you have mastered the basics, I will have you do it again with the practice daggers. Now come on! On your feet!"

With much grumbling, both Gwyn and Tinker get up off the ground, and on shaky legs, stand how Larson shows them, with their feet shoulder-width apart and their bodies centered. He runs them through several foot exercises. First, how to slide backwards and to either side while staying on their toes. Next, he does the same thing with forward motion. Once they learn the foot motions, he drills them by calling out a direction and having them execute it in an instant. Satisfied with their progress, he calls an end to the training for the day.

"Great job, guys! You made it. We will do the same thing

tomorrow. Now I must go to the village. I will be back in the morning for our next workout," Larson says with a wave as he walks off toward the village.

With great effort, Gwyn and Tinker go into the cottage and take turns washing up for the day. They go to the village and sell what they can of the healing potion. When they return home for the day, Tinker once again extracts venom from Cuddles' tail. Gwyn goes out and cares for Dawn Star, whom she has started to just call Starry for short. They get ready for bed, feeling stiff and sore, but ready for more training for the next day.

As the weeks go by, Gwyn and Tinker improve in their training. They can both wield a dagger, and Gwyn can hit a target with ease with a bow. They now look forward to their morning training. Gwyn has opened up more to Larson and tells him she was once married, but is no longer with him. She is feeling more comfortable with him and is allowing him to get closer. As they train, he finds moments to touch her. Either to move her hand or turn her body into a new stance. These touches linger longer than necessary, but Gwyn does not push them away. She has never had someone who treated her well. Her husband always had a cruel hand and a sharp tongue, whereas Larson is kind.

She feels herself falling for him, and she feels like Larson is doing the same. He stays longer and longer at her cottage just so he can be around her. They talk about everything and anything as Gwyn makes healing potions for the journey. But he never stays the night. He is always respectful towards her and tries to help as much in the preparations as possible.

Larson starts traveling to the river every few days collecting the water for them, so they do not have any chance encounters with the mist bears. On one of his trips, he returns with news of the herd that lives in the forest.

"Looks like the old stallion has lost his herd. I saw a young stallion with fresh battle wounds, and no sign of the older one."

"It was bound to happen at some point, but I hope he is safe and not hurt too in the fight," Gwyn says, remembering the stallion's proud look the last time she saw him in the woods. "I just hope he can survive the winter. Next time you go, take some of these apples and leave them for him so he can heal and make it through the winter."

"I will do just that. Now, onward to our training. Today, I am going to add a few additional steps to your defensive footwork," Larson says, setting down the large water skin filled with river water and walking out the door.

Chapter 10

Throughout the winter, Tinker fills up the green potion bottle with Cuddles' venom and gives it to Gwyn to make a salve. All they need is a petrified blossom, which they can get on the way to Inaslas when they cross through the Forest of Stone. Spring is close, and Gwyn has packed all the dried plants and seeds for the move. They purchase a cart for Starry to pull. They also purchase some pots to grow various plants that they find along the way. With the help of Larson's enchanted stones being sold, along with the potion, they have saved up a large sum of gold to purchase a shop when they reach Inaslas.

Gwyn was just putting the last of their belongings into the cart when Larson walks around the corner of her cottage. He waves to her as he walks up and then holds out a small bundle in his hand. Gwyn reaches out and takes the bundle. Looking at him, she opens the bundle. Inside is a small necklace made of fine silver. Hanging on the necklace are three tiny teardrop-shaped vials. In each vial is a different stone chip. One contains a ruby, one a sapphire, and the last an emerald. Gwyn looks up from the bundle to Larson.

"What is this?"

"Remember, I said that I was going to make enchanted items for locating? Well, this is the first one. It is a necklace with chips already primed for the person it can locate. I will need a drop of your blood and a lock of hair to complete it. The same for Tinker. I have already given him his. If you will go inside with me, we can complete the enchantment," says Larson.

"I would be delighted to go inside with you. Come, let's finish this enchantment and see if it works," Gwyn says with a broad grin.

With a small smile and a slight blush, Larson walks behind Gwyn into the cottage. They gather around the table, and each places their necklace on the table. In Tinker's vials, there is a ruby, a sapphire, and a diamond chip. Larson has a sapphire, emerald, and diamond chip in his vials.

"So, you see each vial there?" Larson asks, pointing out each distinct combination of vials. "Each chip represents a person. The emerald chips are for Tinker, the rubies are for me, diamonds are for Gwyn, and Cuddles has sapphires."

He looks at each of them to make sure they understand so far. When they nod their heads, he continues.

"Now I want each of you to take a strain of your hair and place it inside of the vials. Tinker, you can do Cuddles' vials."

They each open the vials on their respective necklace and place some hair strands in the vials with their stone color. Tinker walks over to Cuddles and ruffles his fur until some loose hair comes off and then places it into the vials for Cuddles. Once done, Gwyn and Tinker turn to Larson for the next instructions.

"Okay, now we are going to each prick our finger and drip one drop of blood into the vial, then seal it with the stopper. Now I dislike the idea of Cuddles being hurt, but this would help to find him if he ever got lost or taken. So just a tiny prick on his toe should be fine, Tinker."

"I don't like this, but I want to keep him safe, so I will do it," Tinker says with a grim face.

He walks over to Cuddles and massages his paw for a moment before he takes a sharp sewing needle Gwyn just cleaned and pricks his toe. Cuddles glares at Tinker, but stays still through the entire process. Tinker takes the two vials and adds a drop of blood to each before rubbing his paw and dripping a little of the healing potion on the prick. Cuddles gets up and with a huff stalks away, hiding under Gwyn's bed.

Next, Gwyn cleans the needle and then pricks her own finger. Adding her blood to her vials, she passes the needle back to Tinker after cleaning it again. Tinker does the same, adding his green blood to the vials and then passing it to Larson. Once they have all added their blood to the vials, Larson holds his hands over their necklaces and begins his enchantment.

"*I call upon the arcane powers of the earth to help bind these stones to the blood and hair given. With this binding, may the wearer find those who are lost to them by calling out the name. May the wearer embrace them and end the search for those lost, now found. May all be bound until their last breath.*"

As he weaves his spell through the necklaces, they glow a bright white. Inside the vial, the hair burns away, and the blood and ash seep into each of the stones. Once the stones absorb the blood and ash, they become vibrant versions of themselves, with each giving off a slight glow that shimmer in the vials. When he finishes the enchantment, he hands Gwyn and Tinker their necklaces and slips his own over his head, letting the vials rest against his chest.

"Now, to activate the spell, all you must do is hold the vial and say 'Find,' and whoever you are looking for. When you find them, all you must do is tap them and the spell ends. Like this: 'Find Tinker.'" As Larson speaks, he holds the vial with the emerald in his hand.

As he lets the vial go, it lifts on its own on the necklace and points towards Tinker with a soft green glow coming from inside the stone. He takes a few steps towards Tinker, and as he does so, the glow gets brighter until he stands beside him and taps him on the shoulder. When he does so, the stone vial stops glowing and drops back down on Larson's neck.

"This is amazing, Larson!" Gwyn exclaims. "Thank you so much for this!"

She walks over to him and hugs him. Larson is stiff for a moment in her arms and then embraces her back. They hold each other a moment longer, and when Gwyn looks up to Larson, he squeezes her tighter in the embrace. He tilts his head down and is about to kiss her when they both hear a cough. They turn to see Tinker staring at them, and they step back from each other, looking embarrassed.

"Well, I think I am going to go to the village and pick up some more potion bottles for our journey. Tinker, could you have all the vegetable seeds packed and make sure we are not forgetting any important herbs or plants? Would you like me to pick up anything for you?" Gwyn says as she picks up her new belt satchel.

"No, Gwynie, I'm fine," Tinker says, looking between them. "Just make sure you get different size bottles, and maybe some small tins so we can put the salves in."

"Okay, I can do that. I will see you in a little while, Tinker. I'm going to stop by the tavern before I come back, so don't wait up for me."

Gwyn turns and heads out the door. As Larson turns to follow, Tinker calls out to him.

"I see what you have been doing, trying to get close to her. I am only going to say this once. Do not hurt her, *or else*."

"I would never hurt her. You have my word on it," Larson says to him, and walks out the door behind Gwyn.

Larson catches up to Gwyn, and they walk side-by-side down the road towards the village. Halfway there, on impulse, Larson grabs her hand and holds it. Gwyn, shocked, looks at his hand. With a smile, she squeezes it as a small blush spreads across her cheeks. Hand in hand, they continue toward the village. Once they reach the village, Larson brings her hand up to his lips and kisses her knuckles.

"Once you are done with your shopping, will you meet me inside the tavern for a drink?"

"Yes, I won't be long. Save me a seat," Gwyn says, flustered, as she turns toward the glass maker.

She has not felt like this in a very long time. Excited, and feeling butterflies in her stomach. Not since she first met her husband. Even though they arranged the marriage, he was so charming in the beginning. Handsome, though a few years older than her, with a quick, witty retort to something someone said. At first, she thought it was funny until he turned those retorts toward her. He knew how to hide the true monster he was inside. She had always felt he was a little off, and that something was not quite right with him when they first met. He had a cold feeling about him, and his smile never reached his eyes. But she went against her intuition and listened to her mother, who said it would be the best match she could ever hope to get. But with Larson, it is different. She has a good feeling about him. One of warmth and kindness.

Chapter 11

Gwyn makes her way to the glass-maker, wanting to speed this task along so she doesn't keep Larson waiting too long. As she makes her way to the end of the village, she makes a note of which shops she needs to stop at on their last day, such as the food-vendor and the general store. When she reaches the glassmaker, she knocks on the door and waits. A short, burly man answers the door, and with a grunt lets her in. She looks around the shop at all the unique creations he has for sale. As she stands there, sweat forms on her brow from the sweltering heat from the furnace that he works at.

She walks over to the shelf with the small, clear vials about the length of her palm and gathers thirty of them. She also collects about twenty amber-colored vials for the agility potion she will make. Gwyn wants to make sure that her potions don't get mixed up with one another. She will need to create labels for her potions. She sees some blue vials on the same shelf and grabs ten of them. These she wants for the paralysis potion she will create. As she turns to go to the counter, she spots a large black glass vial on a shelf by itself. It is large and round at the bottom. As the stem goes up, it twists with a grayish highlight. On a whim, she grabs it as well. She doesn't know what she will use it for, but she likes the look of it. Later, she can figure out what to keep in it.

She pays for her potion bottles and then makes her way to the blacksmith to ask for several tins to be made for the paralysis salve. She wants to make both a liquid and topical form of it. The smithy tells her he will have the tins ready by late evening the next day. She pays him for the tins and then leaves, making her way towards the tavern.

When she walks in, she waves to Joslyn, who is at the bar, and spots Larson in the back corner at a small table. She walks over and sits down, and he waves Joslyn over. After a moment, she comes over and asks for their order.

"I would like a pint of ale and a bowl of your famous potato stew," Larson says with a smile.

"What about you, Gwyn?" Joslyn says, turning to her.

"Oh, I will have the same thing. Your stew is my favorite." Gwyn laughs as she settles more comfortably in her chair.

"All right, I'll have everything ready and brought to you in a moment," Joslyn says, breezing back over to the bar to get the drinks.

When Joslyn returns, she sets the drinks down with a pitcher full of ale and a platter of meats and cheeses. With a wink to Gwyn, she walks away and into the kitchen in the back of the tavern. As they wait for their stew to come, they sip their ale and nibble on some of the food on the platter. Once Joslyn brings the stew to them, Larson breaks the silence.

"So, how was the final shopping trip? Do you think we have enough for our journey?"

"Yes, I think I have everything. The blacksmith will have the tins ready tomorrow evening. I want to get our food rations on the day we travel, so the food is fresh as possible. Also, we can always pick up more supplies when we pass back through on our way to Inaslas. Do you have everything you need for the journey?" Gwyn asks him around her spoon of stew.

"I have everything I need. My crystal supply is getting a little low, but once we reach Inaslas, I can visit a vendor and purchase more, or travel to the Cave of Glass and collect some myself."

"Have you always wanted to be an enchanter and to enchant stones?" Gwyn asks, taking a large drink of her ale. The cook has been a little heavy on the spices for the stew tonight.

"Ha, yes, I have. I came from a very poor village far south from here in the Scrubbed Desert. I always had a knack for enchantments, even at a young age, and as I got older, I would sell my stone to help put food on the table. It was just my mother and my younger sister."

"What happened to your father?"

"A sand drake killed him. It came into our village after our livestock, and my father went with the other men of the village to save them from the drake. He and another man were killed, but in the end, the other men of the village slew the beast. They presented one claw of the drake to my mother in a show of respect for losing her husband."

"I am so sorry to hear that about your father," Gwyn says, setting down her spoon and reaching over to hold his hand across the table.

"It's fine. It happened a long time ago. I had to learn to be a man fast, so I didn't have time to feel sorry for losing my father. After all, I had my mother and sister to look after."

"If you ever want to talk about it, I am here to listen, okay?"

"Okay," he says, squeezing her hand, then letting go to finish his stew.

They eat in silence for a few moments, and Gwyn changes the subject to lighten the mood.

"So, what is the Scrubbed Desert like?"

"The Scrubbed Desert is quite fascinating. It has reddish, tan-colored sand with large, craggy mountains. The plants are very scraggly because of the dry and somewhat cold climate. The desert is hot during the day, but the temperature drops at night."

"And how do you live in such a climate?"

"Well," Larson begins, taking a large swig of his ale, "we live in a cave system that was cut into the mountains a long time ago. It helps shelter us from the weather, and keeps us cool during the day and warm at night. There is an entire city built into caves with layers of individual homes built for each family. The only real dangers are rocs and sand drakes. They can slip in through the large openings at the top of the mountain that are carved out for collecting rainwater and air circulation."

"It sounds fascinating. I hope to see it someday. Maybe you could take me and introduce me to your family," Gwyn says with a shy smile.

"I would love to. You would love the view of the stars at night through the open spaces. It is like looking at a picture, but so much more," Larson says with a far-off expression and a wistful smile.

"I was watching how you enchanted our necklaces. Is that how you do all the enchantments for the stones and other items you enchant?"

"Well, come upstairs to my room. I can show you some items I am working on and some materials I use for my enchantments," he says, standing up and reaching out his hand towards her.

Gwyn takes his hand, standing up, and follows him up the stairs where the rooms for rent are in the tavern. They make their way down the long narrow hall and stop at the second door to the end. Larson takes out a key and unlocks his door, opening it for Gwyn to step through. As she walks in, she looks around the cramped room. It has a small bed tucked into the corner with a stand that holds a simple wash basin on it. On the other side of the room is an old beat-up dresser with a bunch of odds and ends on it.

She walks over to the dresser to get a better look and sees that it holds various stones and ingredients. There are also some weapons sitting on the dresser, with various runes and markings inscribed on them. As she inspects the items on the dresser, Larson comes up beside her and picks up a short sword with an intricate design running down the blade.

"This is what I am working on now. I am trying to put an enchantment on it so that it will ignite to help with fighting tougher-skinned monsters. I almost have it. The enchantment on the blade is still being worked on. It will ignite, but only for a few seconds and with a very weak flame. It is something to do with how I wrote the inscription." Larson passes the sword to Gwyn.

She takes it and studies the inscription down the blade. Everything is there for the scribed enchantments to work, but it looks like it needs something else to help boost the power. As she looks from the sword back to the dresser with the gemstones, one stone catches her eye. It is a rough-cut garnet about the size of a thumbnail. She reaches over and grabs it, then hands it to Larson.

"What about this? Could you use the stone to amplify the power of the enchantment?"

Larson, taking the stone, inspects it, then takes the sword back from Gwyn and studies the pommel. He sits down on his bed, and taking a carving tool, makes a small indent into the wooden pommel and places the stone in it. He next finds some copper wire from the supply box he keeps under his bed. Taking the wire, he binds the stone in place, and using a simple spell, he enchants the stone to be a channeler and amplifier of power.

He stands up and motions for Gwyn to stand in the far

corner, out of the way of the blade's swing. He gives the sword a few test swings to make sure the stone will stay in place. Satisfied it will stay in place, he then says the word, "*Ignite,*" and the sword lights up with fire, starting from the shoulder of the blade to the tip of the sword. The fire is burning a vibrant orange and red color and Gwyn can feel the heat coming off the blade from where she stands in the corner.

Larson gives the sword a few more test swings, and seeing that the blade stays on fire, he waves his hand up the blade and the fire extinguishes. Looking up from the sword, he locks eyes with Gwyn, and taking two huge strides, he sets the sword against the wall. He pulls Gwyn into an embrace and kisses her. Gwyn, in total shock, freezes for a moment. She is at war within herself. Her past rears its ugly head. She feels trapped with him pressing her against the wall, but she also wants to break free and embrace him back.

He feels her stiffening and pulls back from the kiss.

"Sorry," he says, looking embarrassed. "I shouldn't have done that, I thought you had feelings for me, too. I apologize for my actions."

"No! I—it isn't what you think," Gwyn says, grabbing his arm and pulling him back when he tries to back away. "I told you I was married, but I never told you what happened in my marriage. My husband abused me. That's why I-I froze and didn't react."

"Now I am sorry. For if I would have known, I would not have acted rashly, and instead asked for permission of my advances." Larson is aghast about what he has just learned. "I never wanted to make you uncomfortable, so please forgive me."

"There is nothing to forgive. It is I who should have told you sooner about my past as soon as I figured out my feelings for you.

Come, let us sit down and I will tell you all about my first marriage," Gwyn says, walking over to his bed and sitting down.

She pats the space beside her where she is sitting, and after hesitating for a moment, Larson walks over and sits down on the other side of the bed, making sure to not touch or crowd her on the small mattress. When they are both settled, Gwyn begins her tale. She tells him everything she told Tinker. How her husband used to beat her and humiliate her. How he would force himself upon her and make her feel worthless. When she is done, she looks down at her boots, not meeting Larson's stare. She braces herself for what is coming; disgust towards her for being broken and used goods, or worse, pity for what she went through.

"Gwyn, look at me," Larson says.

When she looks up and meets his eyes, she doesn't see pity or disgust. She sees pride.

"What you went through was horrendous, but you survived. Few people could have gone through what you did and come out stronger. You didn't let him break you. I am so proud of you. Look at all that you have achieved after fleeing him. You created a potion that heals faster and better than any other out there. Not only that, but you also have ideas to create even more. So, never feel sorry for yourself or embarrassed about your past, because not only did you survive, but you are now thriving."

As he speaks, he reaches out and wipes away the tears now streaming down her face. He then reaches out and holds her close to him as she cries. She cries for a while and when she finishes, she pulls out of his embrace. Giving him a watery smile, she stands up.

"I need to head back before it gets too late. I think we should leave tomorrow after we pick up the tins from the blacksmith. Do you think you could be ready by then to leave?"

"Of course," Larson says, standing up as well. "I will walk you home and then return to pack what I have. Let's meet at the general market tomorrow and get the last of our supplies."

"Okay, let's get a move on then," Gwyn says as she turns towards the door.

They both make their way down the stairs in silence, neither wanting to speak. Gwyn waves to Joslyn as she leaves and walks down the road towards her cottage. When they arrive, Larson bids her good night and turns to return to the Drunken Dragon, but she stops him. She stands on her toes and gives him a quick peck on the cheek. Blushing, she hurries inside and closes the door. Larson stands there for a moment, and smiling to himself, turns and makes his way back to his room. Dawn will come sooner rather than later, and he wants to be prepared to leave.

When Gwyn comes in through the door, she places the vials she has purchased on the table. She tells Tinker her plan to leave tomorrow after they pick up the tins, and that they are meeting Larson at the general store. They both spend the next few hours packing the rest of their stuff. Double checking that nothing important is forgotten when they finish packing. They settle into bed, and as they both drift off to sleep, Gwyn thinks about Larson and the kiss they had shared. With a burning blush on her face, she drifts off to sleep with dreams of Larson, and of what could be between them if she can just find the courage to face it.

Chapter 12

"I think that's everything, Gwynie," comes Tinker's muffled voice from under Gwyn's bed.

He slides out from under it, checking one last time to make sure they haven't missed anything. Standing up, he dusts himself off and walks out the back door.

"Did you hear me?" he asks, walking up to Gwyn, who is tying down the last of the plants they are taking with them.

"No, sorry, what did you say?"

"I said, that's everything. The cottage is empty."

"Good, let's go then. I'm excited to get the new chapter of our lives started. And the sooner we get to the coast, the sooner we can create our new potion," she says, climbing up onto the cart and adjusting the long reins connected to Starry.

She reaches down and helps Tinker up onto the seat beside her. He turns to check on Cuddles, who is now in a large, square wooded cage. Over the winter, the little orange kitten has grown very large, even for a normal cat. Being part-manticore has caused him to grow to a large size. But as he is part-regular cat, he will never get to the full size of a manticore. He stands two feet at the shoulders, and the quills on his back are half a foot long now.

Once Cuddles is secure, Gwyn flicks her wrist and clucks her tongue, signaling Starry to move. With a huff, he moves forward; and with a lurch, they start on their way to Lancegate. Gwyn turns and gives the cottage that she has called home for the last two years one last look.

"Don't look back at your past, Gwynie; look forward to your future," Tinker says with a smile.

Gwyn looks at him and smiles back, and with a nod, looks forward to a bright new future. They are on their way. First the coast, then the capital.

Starry pulls into Lancegate, and Gwyn guides him over to the blacksmith. She stops him and then hands Tinker the reins.

"I will be right back. Keep a lookout for Larson until I get back."

Gwyn jumps down from the bench and walks into the smithy. Heat hits her from the forge as she approaches the blacksmith. He is hammering on a sword when he sees her. He throws it into a barrel of water and wipes his hands on his smock.

"I have your tins for you, missy," he says as he makes his way over to a small box near the back wall.

He shuffles back over to Gwyn and hands her the box. She opens the box and peeks inside. There are many tins with screw tops on them, about three inches around and two inches tall.

"They are perfect. Thank you so much. Do I owe you anything else for them?"

"No. We are all settled. You have a good day, missy," he says, shuffling back over to his sword and placing it into the forge to heat again.

Gwyn walks out of the smithy and places the box in the back of the cart. She ties it down to make sure it doesn't slide around, then gets back on the bench with Tinker. He hands her the reins, and they set off again through the village. Once they reach the general store, Gwyn once again hands the reins to Tinker and walks into the store, grabbing last-minute items for their trip.

She gets three hard cheese rounds, five hard loaves of bread, a glass jar full of fish for Cuddles, and a few smoked meats. There is a shelf in the back with books stacked on it. Curiosity takes over, and she goes to inspect it. It is an old spell book for simple spells and enchantments. She flips through a couple of pages and adds it to her pile of goods. She continues to grab a few more items, such as different bolts of cloth, some canned goods, and an extra blanket. Feeling satisfied with all her selections, she purchases them and has them boxed and put on the cart.

As Gwyn walks out of the shop, she sees Larson walking over to them with a large sack over his shoulder. He also carries his bow and the sword that Gwyn helped him with the other night. When she sees the sword, she glances away, blushing as she remembers what had happened last night. When Larson stops in front of her, he plants a light kiss on her cheek and then loads his sack into the cart. He slips a small strip of dry meat into Cuddles' cage, and as he climbs onto the bench, he ruffles Tinker on the head, causing his hat to go askew.

Fixing his hat, Tinker glares up at Larson.

"What is wrong with you?"

"Nothing. I am just excited to get this journey started," Larson says, chuckling.

Gwyn, smiling to herself, climbs up and sits on the bench as well, putting Tinker in the middle. She grabs the reins from Tinker again, and with a swift flick, gets Starry going. They make their way east towards the coast. It will be a long journey of about a week until they arrive. But it will be worth it when she gets the feathers she needs for her next potion. As they go down the road, they ride in silence, each one in their own thoughts about this big move. Gwyn, holding the reins in her hand, lets her mind wonder.

"I wonder what type of shop I will buy once I get to Inaslas," she thinks to herself. *"I would like a shop with a big front window and a bright red door to draw people in. One with a home over the top so I can save on money."*

She smiles and continues to imagine her shop.

As Gwyn is thinking about her shop, Larson turns to Tinker and starts asking questions about where he lived.

"I lived in the Venom Bog. It is a large swamp area to the far west, with very poisonous water and giant trees with roots that look like cages or caves. There are many creatures there that live both in the water and in the trees. The ground is sludge."

"If it is sludge, how to you move around?" Gwyn asks, jarred out of her thoughts.

"We built platforms and walkways to cross over the soggy land and water. Our huts are on stilts raised high above the water or built into the trees themselves. If we didn't build them so high, it would flood us out during the rainy season."

"That sounds kind of perilous. Do you have a bridge system to connect each house together?" Larson inquires, intrigued by how Tinker used to live.

"Yes, we have a bridge system that connects each house together across the bog. We also have small, slim boats to navigate the water with when we cannot use the walkways. Now, we have fish for our food. Fish are immune to the toxins in the water and safe to eat. But you must be careful when you fish, because there are swamp dragons and bog cats who want what you just caught."

Tinker continues to talk about his life in the Venom Bog, with Larson sharing some of his life with Tinker. It is late evening when they stop for the night. Larson and Tinker have both shared their lives, and once they pull off the road and get settled for the night, Gwyn shares some of hers. As they sit by the fire eating, Gwyn clears her throat.

"I grew up at the Bix vineyards, far to the northwest. It is a beautiful area. As far as the eyes can see, you can see grapevines. As you know, my father is a winemaker, and a very good one at that," Gwyn says. "He would let me help go out into the grape fields and check to see what grapes were ripe enough to make wine. I lived in a large manor with sixty acres of land. When I was old enough, they gave me a horse, and I would ride all over our property, helping my father. I loved working with my father, but my mother had other plans for me. She wanted me to have a high-status match, so instead of being out in the field with my father, I was stuck in the manor all day with studies and etiquette training." She sighs.

For a few moments, she pokes at the fire.

"That was when I met my husband. Our first meeting was arranged by my mother, and I was married after that, and the rest is history."

"Would you ever go back home?" Tinker asks, stretching out on his blanket and getting comfortable.

"Yes. Yes, I would. Once I have made enough to pay back my dowery and be able to absolve the marriage. I also want to see my father again. I miss him. He was against the marriage, saying he was too old for me, but Mother would have nothing else but me being married off to a member of the Senate. That is why I am trying so hard to make new potions to sell, so I can set myself free."

"Well, don't worry, Gwyn, we will help you and you will never have to deal with him again," Larson says, yawning.

As the fire crackles, Gwyn takes the first watch while the others drift off to sleep. She volunteers because she cannot sleep after talking about her past. As the hours tick by and it draws near to midnight, she feels her eyes grow heavy. She gets up, stretches, and then walks over to Tinker. She shakes his shoulder to wake him, and once he is awake enough to stand watch, she herself lays down on her blanket and falls into a restless sleep.

Gwyn feels someone shaking her shoulder, tensing as she turns from where she was lying to see Larson leaning over her. The sun is just rising, and the sky is streaked with the colors of dawn.

"Hey," he whispers. "It's time to wake up. We need to get going so we can make good progress for the day. Tinker already fed Starry and I am getting ready to hitch him back up the cart. Here, eat this."

He hands Gwyn a sandwich of cheese and dried meat, then stands up and walks toward Starry. Gwyn eats her sandwich as she watches Larson hitch Starry to the cart. Once she finishes eating, she makes sure the fire is out. Tinker is already sitting on the bench looking bleary-eyed, but he still smiles at her as she climbs up beside him.

"Why don't you lay in the cart and sleep for a while, Tinker?" Gwyn suggests, watching him try to hold back a yawn.

"No, I'm fine. I will stay up a little longer."

"Okay. But whenever you are ready, just climb back there and nap. We will wake you around lunchtime if you sleep."

By that time, Larson has already climbed up on the bench with them, and he takes the reins and starts Starry on their way. Tinker manages about two hours more before he takes a nap. As he sleeps, Gwyn makes some of the spare cloth into a harness for Cuddles. She feels bad that they cooped him up in the cage all day, but she fears he might run off exploring and get hurt if she were to let him out on his own. So, Gwyn comes up with the idea of a rope and harness, so that he can explore and stretch without wandering off and getting lost.

When they stop at midday, Larson wakes Tinker while Gwyn sets the lunch out. She shows Tinker the harness she has made for Cuddles, and he is ecstatic. He slips the harness on and lets Cuddles out of his cage, but the cat is not very pleased with his harness. As soon as Tinker sets Cuddles on the ground, he flops over and lies on his side. Gwyn brings over some dried meat and lures Cuddles into walking with it. Once he is used to the harness, they attach the rope and let Cuddles stretch out and walk around, but they never take their eyes off him. They want to make sure he doesn't get wrapped up in the rope or the harness, get caught on something, or get hurt.

Once they eat and give Cuddles about an hour out of his cage to roam around, they pack up and start on their way again. As they carry on, Gwyn remembers the book she bought. She reaches into the back of the cart and rummages around until she finds it.

"Here, I saw this at the store and bought it for you."

"You got this for me?" Tinker asks, inspecting the old book of spells.

"Yes, I thought you wanted to try magic that differed from your own enchanting magic. And if not, then at least you have something to read for the long trip. I will grab my alchemy book once we stop again and read it for new potions. Soon, I will have to do more advanced potions than the ones I have planned," Gwyn says, shrugging her shoulders.

"Thank you so much, Gwynie! I will try it. And I would also like to read your alchemy book as well. The more ideas, the better if we want to succeed."

They continue onward, making their way to the coast. Hopefully, nothing too exciting will happen once they get there.

Chapter 13

They have been traveling for days when they smell the briny scent of the ocean. The travelers know they are getting close and stop for the night. They want to be fresh for when they reach the shore, and set up a camp to wait for the squalls to come for mating season. As they set camp for the night, Gwyn gets Cuddles out and attaches his rope to the cart. After days of being in the harness, Cuddles is used to it and enjoys his moments of freedom.

Gwyn cannot not wait to get a shop, though; she knows he is tired of being cooped up in his cage, and the rope and harness only go so far in allowing him to stretch and exercise. She places his bowl of food in front of him and makes her way around the cart to where Larson is trying to get a fire started.

"Wait, I can do it!" Tinker shouts, holding his right hand towards the pile of tinder on the ground.

"No! Wait—" Larson begins.

But it is too late. Larson is too slow to get out of the way when a huge fireball strikes the kindling and a small inferno engulfs everything around it. Dawn Star rears, trying to get away from the flames, and Cuddles is so terrified, he puffs up his back and shoots some quills in alarm.

"Quick! Grab the water skins. We need to put this out before it gets out of control!" Gwyn shouts, grabbing the first skin she can get her hands on and dodging quills flying in the air.

Gwyn and Larson move and extinguish the fire while Tinker flips through the pages of his book.

"I could have sworn I did that right. Why was the fireball so large?" he says, scratching his head and rereading the spell. "I should have—hey, what are you doing?"

Gwyn has snatched the book out of Tinker's hands and throws it into the back of the cart. That's when she notices that instead of the drinking water, they have used the river water from the Crystal River to put the fire out. Angry, she storms to Dawn Star, trying to calm him down. She walks him up and down the road for a few moments until he calms once more, and then stakes him on his picket line to eat and relax. As she tends to Starry, Larson walks over to Tinker.

"I appreciate you wanted to help me, but do not do spells you are not sure of. It could get yourself or others killed."

"I know that, but she didn't have to snatch the book out of my hands!" Tinker huffs, turning towards Gwyn.

"Please don't talk to me right now, Tinker. I'm glad you are studying, but because of your actions, we are now out of the blessed water for the healing potion. Let me calm down first."

"I'm sorry, I didn't know it would happen like that. I picked the wrong spell," Tinker says, looking down at the ground.

"She knows, Tinker. Just give her some time." Larson sighs, then starts the fire again, and gets the food ready to cook.

A few hours go by in strained silence. Larson cooks and Gwyn is tending to the animals and getting a few supplies ready to collect the feathers and create the potion. She sits down for dinner after packing what she needs and grabs the bowl Larson hands to her. She takes a few bites, then looks at Tinker.

"Tinker, I'm sorry for snatching your book. I saw you studying and practice these past few days, but I didn't expect you to try such an advanced spell like fire casting so soon."

"No, I'm sorry for doing the spell. The training I had

growing up made me think I was ready for such a spell. This magic is easier to learn and cast than goblin magic, which is transformative spells and enchantments. I just got ahead of myself. I will try a simpler fire casting spell next time than the more advanced one. And hey, at least I didn't try the wind spell. I was practicing too to put the fire out," he says, chuckling and grabbing another helping of the stew Larson made.

"Yeah, me too." Gwyn chuckles and clinks her bowl to his in a salute.

They both smile at each other and finish their dinner. The three of them make a plan for the morning as they clean up. They decide that once the day breaks, they will reach the waters where the squalls will nest. They will need to be careful walking through the tall beach grass so as not to disrupt the nests. Tinker will go through the grass, since he is the smallest and will go through it easier. He will collect as many feathers as he can. While he does this, Gwyn and Larson will go to the surf and collect shells, driftwood and other items they can find for other potions and enchantments for the future.

Larson has their first watch this night, so Gwyn and Tinker drift off to sleep. Once it is midnight, he switches with Gwyn, letting Tinker get the most rest so he can be of sound mind dealing with the squalls. When dawn breaks, they all get up, eat a quick breakfast, and then move on to the coast. Gwyn dozes in the back while Larson drives the cart.

Once they reach the coast, Tinker shakes Gwyn awake, and they all gaze out at the ocean. It is a brackish gray color, with sand a whitish yellow. The sea grass is like an ocean itself. Twisting and waving in the wind, the tall tan straw-like grass stands about waist-high to Gwyn. They guide Starry close to the shore and stack him on his line to graze. Gwyn gets her sack she packed yesterday and hands it to Tinker. He sets off straight away into the tall grass to collect feathers.

The squall mating season is in full swing. There are blurs of purple and tan streaks flashing around. Those streaks are the male and female squalls performing their mating ritual. They zip back and forth in mock chases, the females moving faster than the males. The females see which of the males can keep up, and once a suitor is chosen, the male has to hoover in the air to show his strength and stamina.

It is an amazing sight to behold. The bold purple of the male squall's plumage and the gentle tan, brown colors of the females. Gwyn just stands and stares for a moment before she continues to the water to collect the drift from the sea. Tinker can barely be seen over the grass, his head bobbing up and down as he stoops to pick up the discarded feathers from the birds. They take a few hours, but they collect enough of the feathers to try the potion and to make plenty more later.

Gwyn has also collected some sea glass, driftwood, and various sea plants that have washed up onto shore. If she can preserve them and grow them at her new shop, it will save many trips to the ocean. Larson also finds some driftwood he deems suitable for his enchantments. He wants to make several staves for mages.

They spend the rest of the day at the beach enjoying wading in the water and just relaxing from their long journey. Tinker suggests they stay a few days so that Gwyn can practice making the agility potion. Since the squalls are there, and it will be easy to get more feathers than just leave and have a limited supply.

Gwyn pulls her small cauldron and the quick seed pods out, along with other ingredients required for the potion she has stored in the cart. Gwyn also throws her bear cloak over her shoulders to shelter her from the brisk ocean wind as she works. She sits on a stump and starts a small fire. Once the fire is ready, she places her small cauldron over the fire, hanging on a spit and filling it with water. Taking the quick seed pods, she splits them open to expose the meat inside. She takes the meat from the pods, and scoring the top, she then smashes them until the oil from the seeds comes out. Placing the oil in a small bowl, she grabs some salt and mixes it into the extract. Making sure it's mixed well, she places the small bowl next to the fire as close as she can and starts baking the salt. As the salt bakes, she takes dried parsley, holly bark, and the petals off a dried brown holly flower, and puts them into her mortar. Taking the pestle, she grinds it all into a fine powder.

Once the salt has finished baking, she pulls the bowl away from the fire to cool while she adds the powder to the water, now boiling on the fire. Stirring the water, she places five squall feathers into a bowl, and taking a small ember, lights them on fire. After the feathers are burned, she adds the ashes to the cauldron and stirs. As the potion cooks, it turns into a golden yellow color. She adds honey for flavor to hide the bitter taste of the quick seed.

Taking the small vials, she has left resting at her feet, she fills one of them up and motions for Tinker to come over. When he shuffles over to her, she hands him the vial of potion.

"What do you think?"

He inspects it for a moment, then he gives it a sniff. Satisfied with his inspection, he takes a sip of the potion.

"Well?" Gwyn inquires.

"I feel normal. Let me test it. Hold on," Tinker says, taking a few steps forward.

As he is stepping forward, each step becomes faster. He runs down the beach, and as he runs, he becomes a blur of green across the sand. The green streak heads towards Gwyn, and at the last moment before collision veers left, now streaking towards the water. He is running so fast he runs on top of the water.

Gwyn can hear him laughing as he runs across the water. She shakes her head and goes back to filling the vials when she hears a loud splash.

She looks up to see Tinker about ten feet away, swimming back to shore. The potion has worn off. Gwyn notes the time it takes for the potion to wear off, also noting that he only took a sip. It was about five minutes from start to finish for that one sip.

Tinker comes up to her and flops down beside the fire. He takes his hat off and wrings it out.

"Well, that was fun. Did you see my pin turns on the water?" he asks, eyes shining with excitement.

"No, sorry. I went back to filling the vials of the potion. I saw the turn you made towards the ocean though. How was the control? Do you feel tired?"

"I feel fine, just soggy," he says, continuing to wring out his hat. "As for the control, it was perfect. I could turn and stop with no sluggishness or my movements getting ahead of me to throw me off. It was like I never took it."

Larson, who watched the whole thing from the bench of the cart, jumps down with a bundle in his hand.

"Here, some dry clothes. Go change before you get sick," he says to Tinker, trying to hide the mirth in his voice.

"Thanks," Tinker says, taking the clothes from Larson.

He walks behind the cart and changes. While he changes, Larson helps Gwyn set up a drying rack to put Tinker's damp clothes on. When they finish constructing the drying rack, Tinker hangs his wet clothes on it and sets sticks close to the fire so he can hang his boots to dry as well.

After everyone has settled, Gwyn goes back to filling the vials of the new potion. She makes several batches, emptying her stock of clear vials. The golden-yellow color of the potion makes her want to display it to the customers. She packs all the potions away in a box where they will not get broken on their return trip to Lancegate.

They eat a dinner of baked fish they had caught from the sea, which Tinker is ecstatic about. He claims that the fish they got out of the sea tastes better than the fish from his old home, where the fish were slimy from the bog water. Once they have finished eating, they all go to bed under the stars near the beach. There is something soothing about hearing the crash of the waves on the shore that makes everyone relax and feel at ease.

In the morning, they spend most of their time lounging by the water and collecting driftwood. Larson fishes on the surf and Tinker collects a last bag of feathers from the tall grass. When the day ends, they make sure everything is ready for the journey home. They don't want to stay any longer because of their excitement. Gwyn has two potions for sale now, and Larson has carved a staff out of the driftwood. They want to get to the capital as soon as possible to buy their shop, get off the road, and have a place to call home.

That night, Tinker finds a mated pair of squalls that Cuddles has caught. The male squall has a broken wing from being captured by Cuddles, and the female has puncture wounds from Cuddle's teeth. Tinker scolds Cuddles, who just looks on with reproach as Tinker mends the wing of the male and gives some of the healing potion to both the squalls. With much begging, Tinker convinces Gwyn to let him keep the mated pair.

"We could have a steady supply when they preen and shed

their feathers."

"As long as you care for them and keep Cuddles away from them," Gwyn tells him as she strokes one squall on top of the head.

"I will, Gwynie. I will make a large cage to keep them in for now until we get to our shop."

Tinker and Larson spend the next hour making a large birdcage out of driftwood. When the cage is complete, Gwyn layers it with the tall grass and sand so that the squalls are comfortable. She places a small bowl she has into the cage and fills it with water.

Once everyone settles for the night and Larson double-checks to make sure they packed everything, they all go to bed. They are ready for the return journey home, and then the journey beyond that, to Inaslas.

Chapter 14

The trip back to Lancegate goes smoothly. But as they get closer to the village, they notice gray smoke coming from the horizon. When they get within sight, the village of Lancegate is nothing but smoldering ash.

"What happened here?" Gwyn asks, trying to hold back tears.

This was her first true home after she fled from her husband, and it is gone; nothing but embers and rubble.

"I don't know. Let's see if there are any survivors," Larson says as he hitches Starry to a post and walks towards the nearest remains of a building.

Gwyn makes her way over to another building, with Tinker right on her heels. They creep through the rubble and find no one. They exit and move on to the next one. For the next few hours, it is the same thing; for every burned remnant of a building they go into, they find not a soul. It is almost like everyone had just disappeared.

When they all reach what remains of the Drunken Dragon, they pause.

"This is the last one we haven't checked yet," Tinker whispers.

They have made little noise the whole time they were searching. Without knowing what happened at Lancegate, they do not want to alert the person who did this.

"Tinker, stay with the cart. It is getting dark. I want to make sure Starry and Cuddles are safe. We will be back after we check the tavern," Gwyn whispers to him.

Gwyn and Larson approach the tavern. They notice that this building is the most damaged. The roof has collapsed, taking the second floor with it. Walls are charred, buckled in places and with some walls completely gone. When they reach the back where the overnight stalls are for travelers, they see they are destroyed as well.

Larson is the first to crawl his way in. Once he finds a safe route inside, he motions for Gwyn to follow. They crawl around, checking every corner they can reach, and find no one. Everyone from the village is gone. It is the strangest thing. Not one survivor, or even bodies of the dead.

They crawl out of the tavern and return to the cart, where Tinker stands stroking Starry's head. He is looking around, but when he spots Gwyn and Larson coming toward him, he relaxes a little. Tinker, who is more strongly attuned to magic, feels a wrongness in this place, as if the very air is decaying around him.

"I think we should leave," he states flatly as he jumps up onto the bench of the cart. "Something is wrong here. It feels like death is clinging to the very air I am breathing."

He is shaking, while he looks around the area again.

"I feel it too, Tinker. There was foul magic used here." Larson climbs up beside him as he speaks. "Even the burn marks on the stores and houses don't seem right."

He reaches down and helps Gwyn climb onto the bench. She grabs the reins and sends Starry towards her cottage with a sinking feeling in her stomach.

"What's going to happen when we get to my old cottage?" she thinks to herself, all the while looking around for any signs of foul play.

Once they reach her cottage, they are relieved to see that it is still intact. They guess that since it is so far off the road and away from the village, whoever did this missed it in their passing. The unhitch Dawn Star and release him into his paddock, but keep all their belongings on the cart. They don't want to be caught unprepared if something else bad happens.

"I think when we go to the Crystal River, we should take the cart with us and just leave from there. I don't feel safe staying here too long, in case whoever has done these horrible things to the village returns," Larson says to them as he collects the water skins. "We will let Dawn Star rest for the night, then push on as soon as the sun rises."

"I agree with you," Gwyn says, letting Cuddles out of his cage. "We need to be careful. Who knows what direction they took from Lancegate."

"I don't think we should stay at all," Tinker interjects. "I have a bad feeling about all of this. There is a feeling of death here, even though nothing was burned."

"Then what would you have us do, Tinker? Dawn Star is exhausted and needs time to rest," Gwyn argues back.

"Can't you give him an invigoration potion or something?"

"No, it would only exhaust him more when it wore off," Gwyn says, staring to get angry. "Look, I know you have a bad feeling about this. I do too. But we can't run Starry to the ground. It's not fair to him."

"I think one of us should watch over him tonight in shifts, like we did while traveling on the road. It would also be a good idea for not just Starry, but to keep us safe as well," Larson says.

"I still don't like the idea of staying here," Tinker says, rolling his bed out and lying down.

Without another word, he goes to sleep with his back to them. Larson volunteers to do the first watch and goes outside to survey the area around the cottage. Gwyn lays down in her old bed, but sleep evades her. She feels restless and on edge. Maybe Tinker is right, and they should have just left straight for the river. It might be safer in the woods, away from the roads.

Around midnight, Larson comes in and wakes Tinker up for the next watch. He lays down on Tinker's bed and dozes, but never truly sleeps, stirring at every sound. No one is getting any rest that night. Cuddles paces around the cottage with his quills up off his back. When early morning comes, they all skip breakfast so that they can leave right away.

They hitch Dawn Star back up to the cart. Tinker just throws his bed into the cart without rolling it up, and they set off. As Cuddles paces back and forth in his cage, they can hear him growling. Larson guides Dawn Star through the woods, and when they reach halfway to the river, they don't even stop. They push forward deeper into the woods, determined to get away from Lancegate as fast as possible.

Once they are close enough to the river to hear it, they stop and tie Starry to a tree to rest while they go to the river to collect the blessed water. Larson stays with the cart as Gwyn and Tinker make the rest of the way to the river. As they creep closer to the river, they notice red streaks dotting the ground. Tinker bends down to inspect a streak and recoils away from it.

"It's blood!" he exclaims, looking at Gwyn with horror in his eyes. "But it's not just any blood, either; it's unicorn blood."

"Larson mentioned a younger stallion taking over the herd. Maybe he was in another fight for dominance?" Gwyn suggests.

"I hope it is that, and not something far worse," Tinker whispers as he creeps forwards out of the trees and towards the river.

The sight of the river is horrifying. There is blood everywhere. It is all over the ground and running in the river, which has lost its crystalline shine, and around the riverbank are

115

the bodies of unicorns. There are about seven dead bodies lying across the forest floor. What is worse is that the unicorns have their horns cut off flush with the skulls, and the skin stripped from their bodies. The blood and gore at the riverbank have a putrid smell of rot and decay. The unicorns have been dead for some time. Other than the horns and the skins, they have taken nothing else from the corpses.

"Who would do such a thing?" Tinker asks, dismayed at the sight before them.

"Poachers!" Gwyn says with disgust. "Poachers will kill unicorns for their horns to grind down for potions and enchantment enhancers. They will also steal their hides to sell to nobles and upper classman who like to wear their shimmery coats for fashion."

"That's horrible!"

"I know, and that's why it is illegal to hunt them now. They are close to being extinct because of overhunting. My mother has a unicorn coat. My father wanted her to get rid of it, saying it was wrong to have one from something so pure and beautiful, but she cried and begged for days until he let her keep it. I always hated seeing her wear it. She claimed she had to keep up with fashion of the upper class and had to look the part of the station she was in."

"I'm starting to not like your mother, Gwynie."

"Yeah, me too. It's because of people like her that something like this happens. And because unicorns are becoming rarer, the hides and horns bring in more money for the seller," Gwyn says, turning away with disgust and sadness from the scene before them.

"What should we do now, Gwynie?"

"I don't know, Tinker. I don't want to leave them here like this, but there is nothing we can do for them now. The least we can do is report what has happened here and at Lancegate in the next town or village. Someone will come to investigate for sure. But for now, let's just return to Larson and the cart and get out of here."

"Do you think Lancegate and what happened here might be related?" Tinker asks.

"It could be, or it could be two different occurrences. But I don't see why someone who killed all these unicorns would also burn an entire village to the ground and take just the bodies of the villagers. If that is even what happened to the people of Lancegate," Gwyn says, starting back the way they came. "All I know for sure is we will have to be extra careful from now on."

"I agree," Tinker says, following her. "I think we should make that paralyzing salve as soon as possible. The more ways we can protect ourselves, the better. There are too many strange things happening right now to not be more prepared."

"Very true. As soon as we get to the Forest of Stone, I will get the flower we need and make it as soon as possible. I would also like to get another bow for myself. That way, both Larson and I have one, and maybe get another spear or two. It would not hurt to have two or three weapons apiece."

As they make it back to the cart, Tinker spots something shimmering in the underbrush. He stoops to pick it up and finds that it is a horn, most likely dropped by the poachers. He tucks it under his shirt to show Gwyn later, but for now he just holds on to it for safekeeping. They make it back to the cart, and upon seeing their grim faces, Larson asks what happened.

"We stumbled upon the unicorn herd and found them all dead. It looks to be by poachers," Tinker answers him with a solemn face.

"How so?" he asks, shocked at the news.

"The horns are gone, and they have all been skinned," Gwyn says, trying to hold back tears.

It is all becoming too much for her. First the village, and now the death of the herd. She hates to see animals being killed for profit or mistreated. Gwyn doesn't enjoy taking a life, and would do so only if it is for food or she is in mortal danger, like the mist bear attack. She believes that none should ever go to waste. Whenever she needed an ingredient from an animal, she tried to do it in the less harmful way as possible, like picking up the feathers from the squalls that had already shed instead of plucking them off of the bird.

Larson walks over to her and holds her tight. She hugs him back, and she feels Tinker hug her from behind. When she looks down at him, his face is shiny with tears. He, too, hates to see animals hurt. That is why he brought Cuddles home and mended the squalls. In his village in the swamp, a lot of the males liked to hunt the swamp cats for sport, to see who could kill the biggest. That was another reason he had been exiled from his village. They deemed him too weak because he didn't want to take part in the hunts with the rest of the males.

"Come now," Larson says, pulling away and leading Gwyn to the bench of the cart. "There is nothing more we can do here."

They all get back on the cart and make their way through the Shrouded Woods. Gwyn lies curled up in the back of the cart, on Tinker's bed, while Tinker tells Larson of their idea to get more weapons for protection and report what happened with both Lancegate and the herd. Larson agrees with him, stating that it would be a good idea to continue their training, and that he will help them learn how to use a spear in self-defense.

As Larson guides Starry onto the main road, he snaps the reins and has him go at a fast trot. They have only had Starry at a walk until now because they did not want to tire him on the long journey to Inaslas. But with recent events, Larson feels the need to hurry to the safety of the next town they come across. The sooner they find people, the better. The road doesn't feel safe to travel on anymore. Larson wants to hire some rangers to travel with them for the rest of the way to the capital.

Chapter 15

They reach a small town called Gainsvin, which lies halfway between Lancegate and Inaslas. It has taken them about half a week to reach it. They tie Dawn Star to a post outside the local Inn and go inside. Larson looks around for the owner to rent a room for them for the night as Tinker and Gwyn sit down at a table in the far corner. He comes back with a key and tells them he will put Starry up in the stall he also rented for the night. When he comes back in, he brings in with him the two cages containing the squalls and Cuddles.

"I talked to the owner and rented us a room for the next two nights."

"Why two nights?" Tinker asks, sticking his hand in Cuddles' cage, and rubbing his ear.

"That is how long it will take for a ranger to get here; I requested a ranger's escort for the rest of the journey to Inaslas. I would feel better knowing we have extra protection on the road," Larson says, sitting down with a groan.

"I wonder if we could get one ranger to go to the Forest of Stone and collect some petrified blossoms for us?" Gwyn ponders aloud.

"Maybe I could even give them an enchanted item as payment, or you could give them one of your new agility potions," Larson says, stifling a yawn.

Rangers are a guild of people that travel all over the land protecting creatures from poachers and guiding lost questors back to towns. A person could hire a ranger for protection when they traveled from one place to the other, especially in the wilderness. Someone could also hire rangers to find plants, animals, and other various items in the woods and bring them back to the questor when one could not go themselves. They were known for their exceptional tracking and scavenging skills. They are whom Larson wants to hire to help them on the last leg of their journey.

It has been a hard journey for all three of them, with little sleep and the constant stress of looking over their shoulders. They order a light supper of meat and cheese with ale. After eating, they go upstairs to the room Larson has rented for them. It is a small bedroom with two twin-size beds pushed up against the wall. Larson sets Cuddles' cage down and Tinker lets him out to roam the room. Gwyn notes the two beds and points it out.

"There are only two beds between the three of us."

"Yeah, sorry, it was the largest room they have for rent right now. I can sleep on the floor if that makes you more comfortable," Larson says, rubbing the back of his neck.

"No, I have my bed out on the cart. I will get it and then everyone will have a bed," Tinker says.

He sprints out the door and down the stairs.

"Well, I should freshen up. The tavern owner said that there is a large tub with heated water. Unless you would like to go first?" Larson asks Gwyn.

"Sure, I'll go first, but I need to get a change of clothes," Gwyn says, heading for the door Tinker had just run out of and making her way out to where they left the cart.

She bumps into Tinker as she walks out of the tavern and tells him about the tub and hot water. He smiles and walks with her back to the cart. Gwyn pulls her bag containing her clothing toward her and grabs a fawn-colored set of pants and a loose green tunic. She also grabs a small satchel containing her toiletries. She is dying to wash and brush her hair. Her hair looks tangled and ratty from the travels. Tinker grabs the red shirt and the pants she gave him last summer. Taking the set of clothes from him so that he can carry his bed easier, they both go back inside to their room. As Gwyn and Tinker were getting their stuff, Larson made his way back down to the dining part of the tavern and as he passes them, he says he is going to feed Starry for the night and grab his own fresh clothing. He grabs a dark purple tunic and some buckskin pants, as well as his straight-razor and some shaving soap. His face is looking haggard from the traveling they have done, with a scruffy beard and unkempt hair.

Gwyn walks into the washroom and turns the water as hot as she could stand it. As the tub is filling up, she strips off her clothes and sits in the tub, letting the water run over her hair. She finds some soap for her hair and works it through her thick waves. Once she has rinsed her hair of all the soap and grim, she washes her body next with a different soap that smells of lemon and cinnamon. After she has scrubbed herself pink, she climbs out and dries off. As she dresses, she runs a brush through her hair, feeling refreshed for the first time in days. She wants to stay in that tub for hours using up all the hot water, but other people are waiting for their turn. Her cottage didn't have running water, let alone hot water, so this is a rare treat for her in over a year.

She exits the washroom and goes back to her shared room. She knocks on the door to let the men know she is coming in and enters to room.

"Whoever wants to go next, the washroom is free," she says, walking over to one of the beds.

"I'll go next," Tinker says, bounding toward the washroom

with his clothes tucked under his arm.

"Okay… I guess I will wait," Larson says, sighing as he sets his stuff on his bed and sits down.

There is a thick silence in the air. It is the first time they have been alone together since he had kissed her those weeks ago.

"You smell nice," he blurts out, turning red in the face.

"What, did I stink before?" Gwyn asks him with a stern look on her face.

"I… uh… what I meant was," he stammers, trying to think of something to say when he notices her trying to hide a smile behind her hand. "You were teasing me just now, weren't you?"

"Yes." Gwyn giggles. "I was teasing you. Thank you for the compliment. I think it was the soap I used. It was lemon and rose scented."

He looks so relieved that she was joking; she feels a little guilty for teasing him.

"Sorry, I didn't mean to tease you like that," Gwyn says to the ground, not looking at him.

"It's okay, Gwyneth. I'm glad you feel comfortable enough to tease me and have fun," Larson says, smiling at her.

He gets up and walks over to her bed, sitting down beside her. He looks her in the eyes and raises his hand up to her face, brushing away a strand of hair that has fallen out of her braid. When she doesn't stiffen or move away from his touch, he leans towards her, tilting her head back. He is about to kiss her when Tinker bursts into the room, beaming and laughing to himself. He freezes when he sees them. Larson springs up from where he is on Gwyn's bed and, grabbing his stuff, says that he is going to wash.

"What was that?" Tinker says, looking from Gwyn to where Larson has gone.

"Nothing. Do you feel any better after your bath?" Gwyn asks him, trying to hide her beet-red face.

"Yes, I feel great after my bath. I have never used hot water before. We don't have running hot water in my village," he says after a moment of studying her.

"You know… tell me if I am overstepping. But do you like Larson?" he asks.

Gwyn's face turns redder at his question. "You, overstep? Never." She laughs. "Yes, I think I do." Thinking for a moment, she reaffirms what she said. "I do like him, Tinker. I like him a lot."

"Okay… I'm happy for you, Gwynie. But if he hurts you, I will turn his ass into a grass patch. And I mean his actual ass!"

Gwyn bursts out laughing and walks over to Tinker, hugging him.

"That I would like to see. If he ever did anything." Gwyn chuckles.

She gives him one more hug and walks back over to her bed, lying down. After a few more moments, Larson returns to the room, clean and shaven. When Gwyn sees him freshened up, she glances away, blushing again. She hears Tinker snickering, and grabbing her pillow, chucks it at him, hitting him across the face. He grabs it and throws it right back at her, but misses, hitting Larson instead.

With a chuckle, Larson grabs the pillow and slaps Tinker across the head with it. Laughing, he dodges the pillow Tinker has on his bed. They throw the pillows at each other and laugh like children for about an hour before they settle into their beds. It feels good to be off the road and not always looking over their shoulders. All their worries melt away, even if it is only for that short amount of time. They drift off to sleep, feeling relaxed for the first time in days.

Over the next two days, while they wait for the rangers to come, they each do their own thing to pass the time. Tinker studies his spell book and practices a repelling spell that creates a shield to protect the wielder. He has Larson and Gwyn take turns throwing stuff at him so he can practice, casting it and testing its strength against various objects.

Larson makes himself busy finishing a staff he has been working on since they arrived from the coast. He has carved intricate designs and symbols all down the shaft and inserted a large smokey quartz crystal into the top to help channel magic. He also helps Gwyn with designing the sign for their shop. She has chosen the colors, but cannot decide on a specific design. She is torn between having a potion flask with the letters "QE" in the middle with crystals around it, or just have it say "Questor's Emporium".

They are all working on their own projects when they hear a knock at the door of their room.

"Yes?" Tinker asks, looking up while blocking Cuddles from escaping. It is the owner.

"There are some people asking for Larson downstairs," the owner says, then turns and goes back down to the main area.

Gwyn and Larson put what they are working on away, and the three of them head downstairs. When they reach the bottom, they spot two men and a woman lounging at the bar. The rangers have arrived.

Chapter 16

The two men and one woman sitting at the bar could be nothing else but rangers from how they are dressed. All are in worn brown leathers, rugged boots, and long black cloaks. But what makes them stand out is that each of them has their own familiar. The older of the two men has a red-tailed hawk sitting on his shoulder surveying the tavern. The younger man has a wolf lying by his feet under the bar, and the woman has the strangest medium-sized cat they have ever seen. It has long greenish-gray fur that trails to the ground, but it looks like it has reeds and water lilies growing in it. When it turns its head towards Gwyn, she sees it has solid black eyes.

"A bog cat!" Tinker squeals, bounding over to it.

He squats down in front of it and holds out his hand. The bog cat gives his hand a curious sniff, then turns to his owner. Gwyn is looking at the cat's owner, too. She is beautiful, with dark, ebony skin and curly, long hair pulled into a tight plait. Gwyn can just make out the points of her ears sticking out of her hair.

So, she is Elvin. Also, judging by the long, slender bow slung over her shoulder and the intricate tattoos running down her arm, she comes from the Elvin City of Rivers, near the Venom Bog. They are known for making the finest vessels for traveling on rivers. The boats they create could travel down any river, no matter how narrow or rough the waters get. Also known for their ingenious constructing skills to control the rivers.

Next, Gwyn looks at the younger of the two men. He is lanky

and looks to be over twenty. From just his looks, Gwyn guesses he hails from the Singing Mountains. The Singing Mountains get their name from the sound that the wind makes as it blows through the peaks. The people who live there are a hardy lot who make the cold peaks their home. Known for the wool they produce from a special breed of sheep. The wool is as soft as silk when spun.

Gwyn looks at the oldest man in the group. He is also the largest. She can tell that he is part-shifter. His height and skin tone give his heritage away. The giant of a man is watching Tinker scratch the bog cat behind the ear and smiling at him.

Larson clears his throat to get their attention. He reaches out his hand toward the Elvin woman first.

"Hello, my name is Larson, and this is Gwyneth. The gentleman petting your bog cat is Tinker."

"Hi," Tinker says, still rubbing the bog cat.

The woman clasps her hand into Larson's and shakes it.

"My name is Eela; this on my right is Jesseph, and to my left is Hardgon," she says, gesturing to first the lanky man, and then the older one.

"So, we received a summons to help some travelers. How is it we can help you?"

"Well, allow me to order us some drinks, and we can sit at a table and discuss our business," Larson says, motioning to a nearby table.

As everyone else makes their way to the table and sits down, Larson makes an order for a pitcher of ale and some food. Once that is done, he comes over and sits down beside Gwyn. He looks at the three rangers again, then begins.

"Well, first I must pass some disturbing news to you. We have come from the village of Lancegate. We returned from the coast to find that the village we live near has been burned to the ground and that all the people in the village were missing."

"What do you mean, missing?" comes the gravelly voice of Hardgon.

"It is just that. They were missing. No bodies, no survivors, and no sign of anything."

"That is disturbing news indeed," says Jesseph in a reedy voice.

"But wait. There is more. We traveled through the Shrouded Woods and came upon the slaughtered herd of unicorns," Larson continues.

"Do you think it is the work of poachers?" Hardgon asks, looking disgusted.

"I don't know. I did not see the herd in question." Larson gestures towards Gwyn. "But she, along with my other companion here, were the ones that found them."

They all turn to Gwyn, and she squirms in her seat. She is just about to speak when the barmaid comes over with their food and ale. As everyone pours drinks and passes food around, she takes a deep breath. She hates being the center of attention. In the past, when attention was drawn to her, a punishment would follow.

Bracing herself, she addresses the rangers.

"I was going to the Crystal River to collect the blessed water for my healing potion. I came into the clearing where the river was and saw about seven dead unicorns. Each one had the horn cut off, and the skin removed."

"So, it is most likely poachers," Eela says.

"From what it looks like," Gwyn says, looking away from Eela's intense stare.

"From these events we have described, you can see why we would like to hire you to help us on the rest of our journey to Inaslas," Larson says, returning their attention back toward him.

"We can take you there. What sort of payment do you have?"

Eela asks, looking at them.

"Along with thirty gold coins, I will give you each an aiming stone, and Gwyneth can give you one of her healing and agility potions each," Larson states, looking between the three rangers. "If you can also get some petrified blossom bulbs, I will throw in an extra enchanted item."

"I think that's a fair trade for our services. We could always use healing potions, and the Forest of Stone is nothing but a small detour on the way. What do you two think?" Eela asks her two companions.

They just nod in agreement and continue to eat their meals.

"Well, it's settled then. I recommend we leave at first light so that we can get you to Inaslas as soon as possible. Then circle back towards Lancegate to investigate what has happened there."

"Sounds good. We will go up and start packing for the journey," Larson says, motioning for Gwyn and Tinker to follow him up the stairs.

Once they reach their room, Larson gets straight to work packing his bag. Gwyn and Tinker follow suit. All three have their stuff packed in no time and agree to turn in early. They don't want to make the rangers wait for them. As everyone lays in their beds, Gwyn can't help but feel a little excitement coming back to her. They will reach Inaslas, and then she can open her shop. And with the rangers' help, she will also have the final ingredient for the paralysis salve. While she lays in bed staring at the ceiling, she smiles to herself and drifts off to sleep.

Bright and early the next morning, everyone gets up and eats a light breakfast before heading out. The journey to Inaslas is thankfully uneventful. But it takes a little longer than the original three days' travel because they must stop and let the rangers check ahead to make sure the way is safe to proceed. On the last day of the journey, Eela parts from them to head toward the

Forest of Stone for Gwyn's blossoms, saying Gwyn will have her flower soon.

They arrive at the gates to Inaslas by late evening on the fifth day of travel. Finding an inn close to the gates, they rent a room for the night. As Gwyn and Tinker settle into the room, Larson pays the rangers and stables Starry.

"In the morning, we will go straight to the senate in the center of Inaslas to apply for our permits for running a shop. We will also look for a shop to buy or rent," Larson says, settling on his bed.. "It is getting too dark to see any of the capital right now, but we can sightsee a little as we look for a suitable location for our shop."

As they settle down for the night, they hear a knock on their door, and Gwyn answers it. Standing at the door is the lanky ranger, Jesseph.

"Here," he says, handing her a small dirty bundle.

Gwyn takes it from him and looks inside. It is the petrified blossom bulbs she asked for, and a few blooms of the flower in the bag as well. She had expected Eela to bring them to her, since she was the one who went to fetch them. But either way, she's glad to get them. When she looks up to thank the ranger, he is already gone. Shutting the door, she walks over to Tinker, showing him what is inside the bag. He gets excited by the sight of the blossoms in the bag along with the bulb.

"We should make paralysis salve right away! We have everything we need now," he exclaims, not able to contain himself.

But Gwyn shakes her head and tells him, "We should wait until we have our shop. Then once we have an actual workspace and not a small room in an inn we can make it the first item we create there."

"Okay, that sounds better actually." He agrees but he can't stop grinning.

They have finally done it; they had made it to the capital. The only obstacle left in their way is to get a shop. They chat late into the night, none able to sleep. Wondering how long it will take to buy their shop and what it will look like. How many customers will they have when they first open it? Gwyn talks about the ingredient garden she is going to have, and Larson describes how he is going to set up his enchantment work area. Tinker comes up with the idea of having an area where they can test out Larson's enchanted items. It isn't until well after midnight that they all fall asleep.

Chapter 17

In the morning, when they get up, they look for the rangers that escorted them to thank them one last time, but cannot find them. The rangers, it seems, must have moved on to investigate what happened at Lancegate. They eat breakfast and go out to the capital. As they walk along the cobblestone streets, they look at the many shops and buildings around them.

They see shops for crafting, and for food. There are places that sell any kind of ware you could think of. As they look around, they see a few empty buildings they hope to purchase for their own shop.

They reach the senate, a large building made of stone, with large oak wood double doors at the entrance. When they enter the building, Larson tells Gwyn and Tinker to stay at the front while he goes and gets the paperwork for their shop. There is a small woman behind him when he returns.

"Hello, my name is Talley, and I will be your guide to purchasing your new shop," Talley says, making a slight bow towards them.

Talley is a pixie. She is maybe three feet tall at the most and has pearly golden skin. She has shocking blue hair and bright purple eyes that twinkle when she smiles. Gwyn thinks she is adorable. She also notices she isn't the only one who thinks she is cute. Tinker cannot stop staring at her. Smiling to herself, she reaches out and shakes Talley's hand. She introduces herself to the pixie and then nudges Tinker to do the same.

"Uh... hi... I'm... I'm Tinker," he stammers, taking Talley's hand.

She giggles at him, but becomes professional again.

"Well, now that we are all acquainted, Mr. Wingdon mentioned that you three are looking for a shop with a two or three-bedroom apartment on top. Is that correct?" Talley says, looking between the three of them.

"Yes, I would prefer at least two, and a nice, spacious area, to create potions and enchantment items in," Gwyn says, smiling. "I also would like to have a back area to grow my ingredients."

"I think I can manage that," Talley says, writing everything Gwyn asked for. "But first, I would like you to fill out these forms, and I will help you fill anything out that you have questions with. Let me pull some flyers of shops that are for sale."

She turns and walks away, giving Gwyn a perfect view of the translucent wings tucked close to her back.

Gwyn finds a table and chairs near the front doors and sits down with Larson. They spend the next hour filling out papers for permits to own and run a shop, and applications for residency at Inaslas. When someone wants to move into the capital, they have to fill out an application for residency. It helps keep the population safe from overcrowding. Whenever Gwyn has to fill out her name, she uses her maiden name of Bix instead of Trueson. She does not want to alert her husband to her whereabouts just yet, not until she has enough to void the marriage.

When they finish filling out the paperwork, Talley presents them with a small stack of flyers of shops. They flip through the flyers and narrow down the stack to two shops. One is on the main street with three bedrooms but no small garden area. The second one has only two bedrooms, and a garden space in the back. But it is on the outskirts of Inaslas. Gwyn, Tinker and Larson talk at length about the two properties and decide on the two-bedroom one. Even though it is on the outskirts, it has an area for Gwyn's ingredient garden, and an attached stable and lot for Dawn Star.

"Fantastic!" Talley exclaims. "I will submit all the paperwork and let you know when everything goes through. Next, let's discuss payment. How would you like to proceed?"

"Well," Gwyn says, looking toward Larson.

She feels like things are moving too fast, but Larson explained to her as they traveled here that they would have to move fast in order to buy a shop before someone else did.

"We would like to pay in gold, if possible," Larson says, looking at Gwyn, who nods her head in agreement. Larson continues. "I think we can put in an offer of five-hundred gold coins. Would that be sufficient?"

Talley blinks for a moment, then composes herself.

"I think five-hundred gold is a fair offer. I will add it to the permit for the purchase of the building. It will take a few days to process, and once the paperwork has gone through and approved, we will seek the payment and then hand you the keys. How does that sound?" she asks them, beaming.

"I think you have yourself a plan," Tinker says, speaking up for the first time since introductions.

Talley giggles at him, and Larson looks toward Gwyn with a smirk on his face, but says nothing.

"Great, it is settled. You can find us at the old inn near the entrance gates. We look to see you soon with good news, hopefully," Larson says, standing up and extending his hand out to Gwyn.

She places her hand in his, and he helps her up, but does not let go once she is standing. Gwyn looks down at their locked hands, then looks him in the eye with a raised eyebrow. He just smiles and leads her out the door, with Tinker trailing behind them.

They spend the rest of the day exploring different shops and cafes. Tinker buys a red silk cord with a gold bell on it for Cuddles. Gwyn and Larson go half each for an extra-large cage for the squalls, and buy more supplies for them. They stop by a carpenter's shop, and Gwyn commissions the design she has decided on for their shop.

She has decided that she wants the sign to be two-feet long, and rectangular with a rounded top to it. She asks the carpenter to paint it bright red, with a gold border going around the sign about an inch away from the edges. The sign will read 'Questor's Emporium' and it will have a potion flask with a crystal inside of it. The carpenter tells her he can have it done in three days, and that he can have it delivered to the inn they are staying at.

They leave the carpenter and continue browsing around the center of Inaslas. They could spend all day looking around and still not see everything inside the capital. Once they are tired of walking, they return to the inn for a light dinner and go to bed after caring for the animals.

The next few days are much of the same as the first, with them walking around and checking out all that Inaslas has to offer. But on the fourth day, they are getting ready to go out again when they hear a knock on their door. When Gwyn opens it, there is a small dwarven boy of about six years old standing with an awkward package in his hands. He hands Gwyn the package and holds his hand out for a tip. Chuckling, Gwyn goes and grabs four gold coins, and gives it to the boy. He stares down wide-eyed at the coins for a moment, then with a quick bow, bolts away without a word. At this, Gwyn laughs out loud, thinking to herself how she was that shy when she was younger. She remembers hiding behind her father and never spoke to the new people being introduced to her. As she walks over to her bed to inspect her new shop sign, there is another knock at the door. Before she can get back up, Tinker bounds over to the door and opens it.

Standing outside is Talley. She gives Tinker a small smile and asks, "May can come in?"

He just nods and opens the door further for her. In her hands is a large stack of papers, and a small satchel is hanging off the sash of her periwinkle dress. When she steps inside, Larson brings over a chair for her to sit on and sits across from her himself.

"Well," she starts, looking at each of them before she continues. "I have the paperwork for the shop, and the good news is they have approved you to buy it. Also, your residency has been approved. I just need you to sign a few papers and then I will put my stamp on it and the shop will be yours."

"Excellent!" Tinker shouts with joy, jumping up and down.

Talley laughs, and when Tinker looks at her, she beams at him, then she looks to Gwyn and Larson.

"Now, payment. When would you like to pay for your shop?"

"We can do that right now," Larson says, going over to where they keep the savings from their wares.

He grabs the coin pouch and hands it to Talley.

"That should be all of it," he says, looking over the paperwork they need to sign.

As he and Gwyn sign the papers, Talley counts the coins to make sure it is all there. Once she and Gwyn and Larson are done, she stamps the papers with the stamp she pulls out of her little satchel, then stands. She reaches her hand back into the satchel and pulls out a large brass skeleton key. She hands Gwyn the key. "Congratulations! You are now the proud owners of your very own shop. I promise to stop by the shop once you are fully open." She says that last part, looking right at Tinker.

His face flushes at her statement, and he makes a goofy grin at her.

"I will leave you all now, and I hope you have a great day. Thank you for doing business with me," Talley says, getting up from her chair and leaving their room.

"Let's pack and go to our new home," Gwyn says, holding the key up and grinning from ear to ear.

They make short work of packing all their stuff, and as Larson pays the innkeeper for the room, Gwyn hitches Dawn Star to their cart one last time. By the time she has helped Tinker get the animals settled into the back of the cart, Larson has returned. They all climb onto the bench and set off.

They steer Dawn Star through the narrow streets until they reach the far-right side of Inaslas. It is the more rural side of the capital, with wider streets and fewer buildings. They pull up to a two-story building standing alone with a small paddock and lean-to on its left side. Larson unhitches Dawn Star and turns him loose into his new paddock. Once he is settled and Larson comes back to the cart, Gwyn walks over to the front door and pulls out the key from her pocket. Looking at Larson and then to Tinker, she inserts the key and turns it until she hears the click of the door unlocking.

She pushes the door open and walks inside. As she looks around the empty, dusty area that is going to be her new shop, she feels tears running down her face. These are not tears of pain or sadness, but of pure joy. Gwyn has made it. She has bought her own shop, and won't have to live under a tyrant of a husband. She will make her own money and finally live her dream as a shop owner like her father.

With tears still streaming down her face, she walks back outside. She takes the sign out of the cart and walks over to the front of the building, where there are hooks so signposts can be hung just over the front door. She reaches up, and with Larson's help, hangs the sign. As it sways in the wind, she turns to Larson and Tinker. Spreading her arms wide, she says,

"Welcome to Questor's Emporium!"